'The Four Fables'

4 short stories

by

Neal Hardin

The Accomplice
The Collector
The Returner
The Stalker

© Neal Hardin 2018
All rights reserved.

Neal Hardin has asserted his rights under the Copyright, Designs and patents act 1988 to be identified as the author of this book.
No part of this book may be reproduced or used, or transmitted in any form, without the prior written permission of the author. For permissions requests, contact the author

This is a work of fiction. Names, characters, businesses, places, events, and incidents are either the products of the author's imagination or used in a fictitious manner. Any resemblance to actual persons, living or dead, or actual events is purely coincidental.

ISBN 9781717862358

<u>To</u>
My former work colleagues and good friends, Marrianne Forbes, Leanne Dolan, Julia Billaney, and Dr Glenn Barr.

The Accomplice

CHAPTER 1

His life changed in the blink of an eye. One minute he was a penniless nobody. The next he had seven and a half million pounds in the bank. He said, rather glibly, that the money wouldn't change him. It did. It changed him in more ways than he ever imagined. His confidence grew fivefold. He became more assertive and sure of himself.

Ray Drummond and I were pretty much cut from the same cloth. Working class guys. Nobodies. Everyday kind of blokes who had to grind out a living working in a soul-destroying office environment. I knew Drummond when he was a skint work-shy gobshite who would avoid doing anything, even in his place of employment. The story of what became of him is a classic example of how new-found fortune can change a life in so many ways and deliver a sting in the tail.

I first met Ray Drummond when we worked together, as account clerks, in the office of a local government authority. Like me, he earned not much more than twelve hundred pounds a month for pushing paper from one tray to the next.

Then one Saturday night his balls dropped. Those six lucky numbers. His birthday 19/5, his mum's birthday 30/12, his dog's birthday 23/4. His six lucky numbers: 4,5,12,19,23,30. The winning lottery numbers that had the power to turn an ordinary, hum-drum life into an extraordinary one. Seven and a half million pounds worth of extraordinary. He had struck it very lucky in a double roll-over.

Sadly, for him, someone else also had those six numbers, therefore the fifteen million roll-over pot was shared fifty-fifty.

He told me on more than one occasion that the money wouldn't change him. It did. How do you win that amount of money and it doesn't have a profound effect on your life? Impossible in the extreme.

By the end of the first four months, after the win, he had done the things most jackpot lottery winners do. He had bought a house in one of the more upmarket and exclusive parts of the town. He had purchased a new car, for him it was two new vehicles. A BMW sports car and an off-road SUV. The kind of vehicles favoured by premier league footballers. He had been on a long-haul trip to some sun kissed exotic location over in the Far East. One thing he did do was to give me, his best mate, a cheque for twenty thousand pounds for which I was most grateful.

I had not heard from him for almost two months, then one night - unexpectedly - I received a telephone call from him. I could sense by the way he was talking that he was restless, or possibly bored with not much to do other than contemplate his wealth. He asked me if I had seen Helen Symonds around town. Helen Symonds was a girl who had worked in the same office as Drummond and me. All the guys fancied her like crazy. She was a beauty, five years younger than us. Tall, blonde haired, slim, bright blue eyes. She was a vision of loveliness. She was way out of our league. She went for tall, rugged blokes and neither Drummond or I fitted the bill. I said no. Why should I have seen her? She had left the place where we worked a few years ago. What was it? Two years ago, at a guess. I had never been close to her or had much time for her. How would I know where she was today? The last I had heard was that she had taken up with a rugby player who played for one of the big London clubs. Anyway, why was he asking? Oh, he said, he was just curious to discover if she was married, had kid's excreta. I could tell that he was more than curious. Perhaps he wanted to find her to see if she was unacquainted. I said highly unlikely. She always had a bloke on her arm. Usually some six feet two, dark haired, muscle bound hunk. Not some five feet something, weedy, average Joe like him and I.

I asked him why he wanted to know about her. He admitted that he wanted to see her. I said okay if that's the case then he had better pay someone who could find her. That wasn't me. I didn't know where she was, and I didn't know anyone who knew of her whereabouts. As I explained it had been two years since she left the office to work in a solicitor's office or some such in the town. She could be anywhere by now.

Drummond asked me what he should do. I repeated that if he was desperate to find her then he had better contact someone like a private detective. Drummond said he would do that. He asked me if I knew anyone? It just so happens that I did. I advised Drummond to contact Tony Plummer.

Tony Plummer owned his own Debt Collection Agency with the ways and means of accessing a lot of information that a normal Joe could never access. I gave Drummond his telephone number.

Drummond contacted him. This is when Drummond's troubles really began.

Tony Plummer got back to Drummond with the information he required. Helen Symonds, now Helen Bovey, lived less than eight miles away from him in a village on the other side of the town. He supplied Drummond with both her mobile and a landline telephone number. He offered to get other information for him, but Drummond said that was enough to be getting on with for now. I guessed how he must have felt when he received the information. Like a voyeur or peeping tom who was about to stalk his prey. He must have felt quietly exhilarated at the prospect of seeing her and discovering how she looked today.

CHAPTER 2

The following day was Tuesday. The morning was sunny but with a bone chilling breeze that went straight through you. Woolly hats and mittens were the order of the day.

Drummond told me that he had set out to find the address where Helen Bovey lived. It took him twenty minutes to drive from his home to the address he had been given. Helen Bovey lived in a big house on a long, tree-lined lane with a narrow dyke running along both sides of the road. Apparently, the road was lined with large, expensive detached houses behind metal rail fences or York stone brick walls. It was exclusive. It was on the edge of suburbia. All mock Tudor fronts, colonnades and first floor balconies. In mid-November, all the roadside trees had lost their leaves so the branches reached up like spindly, grotesque fingers pointing upward. Carrion sat in the trees, lamenting the approaching cold snap. The ground was moist with dew and there was a stinging coldness in the air. The smell of autumn, fallen leaves and damp, was all around.

The Bovey house was a detached property set behind a six feet high brick wall. A red tiled roof with tall chimneys. According to Drummond it was a two million-pound plus home without a doubt. Five bedrooms for sure. A double wooden entrance gate with brick pillars at each side topped with a globe like glass bowl. An intercom unit was embedded in the pillar.

Drummond told me he went by the gate for about fifty yards then did a U turn, then slipped onto the grass verge by the side of the road and killed the engine.

Twenty minutes passed with no sign of anyone emerging from the property. He was on the cusp of leaving when one of the gates opened and a figure emerged. Low and behold it was her. He could hardly believe it. Seeing her for the first time in over two years. What timing. She ambled towards his car, with her head down, just casually walking a big Golden Retriever dog on a long leash.

As she came level to his vehicle she glanced at it fleetingly. A vehicle of this size, in this part of the world, was nothing new. Drummond could see that she hadn't changed much in the time he had last seen her. Her hair was still long and flowing. Her face exquisite. The blonde had turned to a more strawberry-blonde texture. She had maybe put on a pound or two around her hips. She was still the beauty he knew back in the day. She was wearing slim fit jeans tucked into red, calf-length Wellington boots. A baggy wool jumper under a green wax Burberry jacket. She was a vision of beauty. If anything, a little bit of maturity made her even prettier.

For a split second he thought about putting the window down, gaining her attention, then saying something on the line of, *'Helen Symonds. I don't believe it. Fancy meeting you out here. How are you?'* But he thought better of it, that might look to much like a manufactured meeting rather than a chance encounter.

He observed her. He had to admit that he felt a twinge of excitement. It was like he was a teenage kid going through puberty. Like an adolescent who had not quite reached maturity and had a crush on the mother of a school mate. It was all wet dreams and fantasy. In that sexual excitement there was a tiny bit of him that felt guilt and remorse. At this stage it was all innocent, but there was no knowing where this could end.

By the time she was fifty yards passed the car, he started the engine, drove up the road passing her house and away from the area. Now that he had seen her again he wondered what to do next, whether to pursue her or to act more rationally and end his obsession before it got out of control.

CHAPTER 3

It was a Saturday night at seven-thirty when Drummond contacted me. My wife, Carol, and I had just settled down to watch Saturday night television when the telephone rang. We had stopped going out on a Saturday evening because a night out was proving to be too expensive. The twenty thousand Drummond gave me had gone on the mortgage to buy this council house we lived in. It was okay but nothing special.

Carol worked for a big supermarket chain in an edge-of-town-shopping development that contained all the usual suspects. Her job was, floor manager, in the chilled food section. She said she liked working there. I thought that was a white lie. In reality, she hated it and couldn't wait to leave.

Drummond slurred his words so he sounded as if he had been on the sauce. He was a bit groggy and incoherent. I could just about make out that he wanted me to meet him tomorrow afternoon in a pub in town we used to frequent after work. I said okay no problem, for all times sake and all that. We could have a couple of jars, have a chat, and put the world to right. When Carol asked me, who had called I said it was my dad asking me if I had heard todays football results because he wanted to know how the local team had got on. Carol didn't like Drummond. She said he was an oaf and an idiot. I said that was a bit strong, anyway idiots don't live in a million-pound house or drive a brand-new BMW. But she had a point. An idiot can still win a game of chance.

The following day, I told Carol I was going to take Jasper, our two-year-old cocker spaniel dog, for his daily walk. I walked into town and met Drummond in the pub. I was startled to see him. He had lost a lot of weight - at least a couple of stones - since the last time I had seen him. He looked gaunt and his eyes had a vacant look. He put his weight loss down to a fitness regime that had him in the gym three times a week doing weights with loads of circuit training and cardio work, along with swimming several lengths of a fifty-metre pool. The weight loss had made him look a lot thinner in the face. It made him look almost ill. But it was quite the reverse. He was fitter than at any time in his life. His hair was now much shorter than it had been and neatly trimmed and styled. His clothing reflected that he no longer shopped in the discount clothing stores.

He told me he had dated a couple of girls in the past few weeks, but neither of them was interested in his charm, charisma or having his love truncheon tickle their tonsils. What he had not lost was his ability to make me laugh with his one liners.

Word had gotten out a long time ago that he was the mystery lottery winner. Word soon got around this town. It wasn't much more than a market town of twenty thousand people. Twenty-five miles away from the nearest large city.

What he told me next gave me cause for concern. He admitted that he had driven to London on several occasions and paid for the services of prostitutes. It was at this stage that I began to worry for my mate. He seemed to have changed – not just physically – but mentally. Maybe he couldn't handle the big lottery win. Maybe his sense of being or lack of things to do was affecting his state of mind.

What he told me next didn't dissuade me from that opinion. He said he had been to the place where Helen Symonds, now Helen Bovey lived, and that he had seen her. He couldn't get her out of his mind. It was driving him crazy. A lost love. The thought of what-could-have been coming back to haunt and traumatise him. I told him to get a grip. To put it down to life's ups and downs. Sometimes you can't always win and have the things you want. I told him that he had to forget about her. He had to move on. I felt as if I was becoming a kind of counsellor and he was my patient. He said he knew, but he didn't. He was just saying it. He was psychotic, and I was concerned.

We had a couple of pints each. We were sitting in a part of the bar that was well out of earshot of the other customers. The noise from the bar and the music drowned out our conversation. This was a good job because what he told me next wasn't for broadcasting. It was at this point that I really began to worry about my mate's sanity.

He told me he had been back in touch with Tony Plummer. He had asked him for more information about Helen Bovey and her husband. It turned out that her husband was ten years her senior. He was a partner in a firm of accountants called, 'Hepson, White and

Bovey'. They had an office in town and a couple of other locations within a ten-mile radius. Apparently, Michael Bovey was the practice tax expert. I said so what? Drummond said that he was concocting a story to meet him. He was going to pose as a potential would-be charity benefactor requesting his advice on tax matters. This would allow him to meet Bovey so he could size him up.

"I'm not with you. What do you mean by that?" I asked.

Drummond's reply left me numb.

"So, we can put him in a box," he replied.

"What kind of box?" I asked.

"A coffin."

"We?" I exclaimed.

"Us," he replied.

"Are you mad?" I asked.

"Yes, quite possibly," he replied coldly.

He was literally barking mad. Something had gotten hold of his soul and was doing all kinds of weird shit with his head. At that moment I considered going to the police to tell them, but I bottled it. I held back in the hope that he would see sense and drop it. He never did. He said he wanted me to help him. Then he made me an offer I couldn't refuse. His house. He said he would give me his house if I helped him. He would show me the deeds. He would transfer the ownership into my name. I will admit that I was interested but told him I would have think about it.

"What's to think about?" he asked.

"Plenty," I replied.

It didn't seem to deter him. "How can we kill Bovey and dispose of his body?" he asked.

I replied that I didn't know. I looked at him and wondered where all this would lead.

When I arrived back home Carol could smell beer on my breath. She asked me where I had been. I told her I had bumped into a couple of the lads on the common and we had gone for a few jars in, 'The Rising Sun', the pub on the estate. We had a blazing row.

CHAPTER 4

Drummond was shown into Bovey's office by a spotty faced clerk. If the truth be told, on first impressions, Drummond was a bit disappointed by Bovey. He expected a lot more from the man who was Helen Symonds bed partner. He wasn't at all good looking. Average at best. Yes, he was neat and tidy, as you would expect of an accountant, but he wasn't exactly a George Clooney look-alike. He didn't fit the bill of what Drummond expected from the man who had swept her off her feet. The only real positive for her was that he must have been wealthy. That made Drummond feel better in himself.

On meeting, Bovey offered his hand, which Drummond took and allowed him to gauge his height. Drummond was only an inch shorter. Yes, he was slim and well maintained. His belt still had several unused holes in it. Bovey smiled. His handshake was limp and that also disappointed Drummond. After all his weight training with the supplements he took, he was far more solid.

The office was also a bit of a let-down. It was decorated with a pastel, flowery patterned wallpaper that looked like something that was in fashion in the nineteen-eighties. High on the wall behind his desk were a number of glass picture frames containing certificates and diplomas, that kind of thing. The room was chilly. There were no radiators on the wall. Just a mobile convector heater that wasn't on. On the corner of the desk was a picture frame. Drummond managed to take a glance at it as he negotiated the tight space. It was a picture of Helen and Bovey together at what must have been a social function. She was in a long low-cut gown, holding a gold purse in hands; smiling at the camera. He was in a kilt complete with ceremonial jacket and sporran. He looked miserable as his smile was manufactured. Drummond had to smile to himself.

Bovey took hold of the back of a straight-backed chair at the client side of his desk. "Please sit here," he said. Then he moved around to his side of the desk and sat in a high-backed black leather swivel armchair. "How can I help you Mister Drummond?" he asked. The tone of a Scottish accent was audible.

Drummond wanted to say: *'I want your wife you son-of-a-bitch and if you want to stay alive you'd better comply.'* He thought better of it.

He took his seat and settled himself. "I have a substantial amount of money." Bovey's face didn't twitch. He retained a deadpan expression. Drummond continued. "I'm *thinking*" – he stressed the word thinking – "of setting up a kind of trust fund for kids in the area who excel in sport. Football, cricket, and the like. I want to know if I did this what the tax situation would be."

Bovey sat back in his fancy armchair and clasped his hands together over his stomach.

"If you set up a charity, that is non-deductible were tax is concerned because in the eyes of the H.M. Revenue and Customs it's deemed to be in the public good." He seemed to know what he was talking about. He was officious and to the point, but without being brusque or condescending.

"Can you do this?" Drummond asked.

"Do you mean, set up a charity?" Bovey asked.

"Yes."

"I can set up a charity with the Charities Commission then set up a company with Companies House as a charitable venture. How much are we talking about?" he asked.

"Half a million," replied Drummond in a deadpan tone.

A nerve under Bovey's eye twitched. "Pounds?" he asked.

"Pounds," replied Drummond. "Is there a charge to do this?" he asked.

"Yes. There is. It will be five hundred pounds to set up the company and that also covers the administrative costs and our charges as well. You will be able to recover this charge as soon as a tax return is completed." His style was polished. His Scottish accent was melodic and smooth, like a fine malt slipping down into the bowels of your belly.

"How would we go about transferring the money?" Drummond asked.

"That's quite simple. First, we would set up the company then register it with the Charities Commission. Then it would be a case of transferring the money into the company's bank account. Of course, the company will require some trustees."

"Trustees?" asked Drummond in a questioning manner.

"Yes. Maybe two or three people who will act as the executers to ensure that it meets the requirements of the companies act and what not."

The more Bovey talked about executers the more Drummond thought that actually this wasn't a bad idea. He would be doing his bit for the local community. Maybe they would name a road after him or a council building or whatever. Imagine that?

"That sounds fine," said Drummond.

"Good," said a smiling Bovey. The meeting had been conducted in an open, friendly manner and in a business-like way.

They continued to chat for a few more minutes about some peripheral matters, then parted with a firm handshake. Ironically; perhaps, Drummond thought that he might like the man. If it wasn't for him being Helen Symonds husband, then he could really have warmed to him.

Drummond left the offices of, 'Hepson, White and Bovey', fifteen minutes after entering.

CHAPTER 5

Drummond told me that three days went by before Bovey got back in touch with him. In a telephone conversation his first question to Drummond was: Had he had chance to think about it? Was he still keen to go ahead? Drummond said he was. If the truth be told the thought of setting up the trust fund, though pie-in-the-sky at first, was now something he had a genuine interest in doing. He was still earning a good return on his investments and making over thirty grand a month in interest. Drummond did insist that it was to be done on the quiet. He didn't want any of this getting out until all the t's had been crossed and the i's were dotted. He didn't want any publicity what-so-ever. Just like he had told the lottery people.

Bovey said he could set it all up in a few weeks, perhaps they could meet for drinks. Drummond said okay. He looked forward to seeing him again.

The second meeting took place in a trendy restaurant in a town twenty miles away. It was all mood music, concealed lighting and fifty-pound bottles of Chateau this and Chateau that. The setting was nice and relaxing. Pretty boys and girls in penguin suits were on hand to serve them their food and drink.

Bovey was slightly more casual in a dress sense then he had been at the first meeting. Gone was the shirt and tie. Now it was a polo shirt and grey canvas like chinos. Drummond guessed that he would have done his homework and discovered that the client wasn't some crank who said he had a substantial amount of money in the bank, but someone who did have a substantial amount of money in the bank.

Bovey had done his research and presented Drummond with a plan. He could set up a company under the name, 'The Raymond Drummond Charity Trust', then register it with the UK Charities Commission. Once the company was established then it was just a case of transferring the money into the charity. Bovey asked Drummond if he had given much thought to how the trust would operate. Drummond said he had. Potential applicants who had shown a skill in a sport would be able to bid for things like equipment and coaching sessions from the countries best coaches and the like. The only two criteria were that the kids were from the local community and from poor homes. It could also extend to local football, rugby and cricket teams who could ask for new equipment and so forth.

"How very noble," said Bovey. "What a tremendous idea." He suggested that a couple of sports people from the local boy's and girl's clubs and the town's professional clubs be brought on board to, one, give the kids the heads-up and also, two, to act as panel members to decide who the lucky applicants are. If they were successful, then the trust would reimburse them on evidence that they had purchased the equipment they had applied for. Drummond went along with the plan. He was happy with the idea and pleased to let Bovey make the arrangements. After all, if you couldn't trust an accountant who could you trust? He did once again insist that Bovey had to keep this close to his chest. If news got out that he was thinking of setting up a charity than he would pull the plug in a heartbeat. Bovey said he could trust him. His integrity was assured. As the meeting came to an end they toasted each other's success, then went their separate ways.

As he drove away Drummond felt a sense of purpose. He loved sport and the thought of giving local kids the chance to shine had struck a chord with him. He was also taking a liking to Bovey. He was coming across as a genuine type of guy. Quite humble. Although he appeared to be financial comfortable he didn't drive a brand-new car. Indeed, the car was several years old. A dilemma was setting in. Suddenly the thought of killing him maybe wasn't such a good idea. Maybe he could make access to Helen through Bovey. Not around him.

One week had elapsed since I last spoke to Drummond. As I had not heard from him I assumed he had gone cool on the idea of murdering Bovey. I put it down to an aberration on his behalf and his off-the-wall Walter Mitty character. Hopefully, he had seen sense and dropped the idea.

Things were not going great in my own life. Carol, my wife, had left me for a couple of days, saying she needed a break from me. She had gone to spend time with her mother. Despite the usual stereotype about mothers-in-law, mine was okay. We got on fine. Carol returned home unexpected early the following day. We talked for hours and just about got our marriage back on the straight and narrow.

It was to be another eight days before Bovey got back in contact with Drummond. He told him that preparations were on track. He had made the necessary application to the Charities Commission and he had taken the first steps in setting up the company under which the trust would operate with the necessary memorandums and what-not. As far as Drummond was concerned Bovey could have been talking a whole new language. He said he understood what he was on about, but in truth he didn't. To progress things along Bovey requested that he come into the office in order that he could sign a, 'Memorandum of Intent'. He also suggested that he write a cheque made directly to him for the half a million pounds. Once the paperwork was complete he would transfer the money into the trusts bank account, which he was setting up with a local bank. This would quicken the process. Drummond said okay but suggested that instead of him going to see Bovey in his office, that Bovey came to his home. Bovey agreed to the idea. After all, if you couldn't trust someone who wanted to set up a charity, then who can you trust?

So, it was that Drummond invited Bovey to his home to complete the paperwork and also to give him a cheque for half a million pounds.

CHAPTER 6

Drummond resided in a house on an exclusive, executive development on the edge of town. The homes were large. They were either four bedroomed or five bedroomed properties surrounded by enough land to put in a second home if the owner wished. Drummond's house had a double garage attached to it with access via an internal door.

He had purchased the house at a knock down price of seven hundred thousand when the agent told him it was worth double that. It had a mock Tudor front over a steep sloping red tiled roof, the remainder was red brick. Imitation shutters at the windows gave it a kind of French chateau style. A climbing frame attached to the side of the house held a thick green clematis bush that covered at least thirty per cent of the brickwork. It needed pruning back. Drummond had asked a local firm if they could do it, they had given him a price and said they could start work in a couple of weeks.

The interior consisted of a large lounge overlooking a back garden that contained a carp filled pond. On the patio was a brick constructed BBQ unit with the latest state-of-the-art grill. Other ground floor rooms were a study, a dining room that could easily accommodate a large dinner party, and a spacious kitchen. There was also a games room. Drummond had bought an oversize blue baize covered pool table. He had also purchased two arcade machines that had cost over twenty thousand pounds each. One was a Formula One game in which two players could race each other around the Monte Carlo circuit in Formula One cars. The room also contained an upright cold unit that contained several bottles of wine, multiple packs of canned beer and soft drinks.

Upstairs there were four bedrooms and two large executive bathrooms both with stand-alone tubs and tall shower cubicles. Down below there was even a cellar which Drummond used for storage. The house was far too big for one person. Drummond knew it, but he wanted to look the part of a winner. It was brash, big, and said look at me.

It was just after eleven o'clock when Bovey arrived for the meeting. He was driving his three-year-old Lexus saloon which he parked in the forecourt by the double garage. He was alone. Drummond met him at the front door. Bovey was casual in the same zip-up sports jacket he had been wearing at the meeting in the restaurant. He was carrying a black leather briefcase in his grip. Drummond greeted him with a smile and a handshake. Bovey looked relaxed and sure of himself. He glanced up at the front of the house, admiring the black and white frontage.

"Nice house," he said in a patronising way.

"Yeah," replied Drummond. "Too big for me, but I do like it," he commented. He invited Bovey into a reception area which had a tile granite floor. Ahead was a wide stairway going up to the first floor. Sets of oak panelled doors led into the rooms off the reception.

The interior impressed Bovey. "Nice colour scheme," he commented. Drummond had had it done in gold leaf wall cover. A Rodin style sculpture stood on a plinth. Light cascading in through the double window at the turn of the stairs was splashed across the naked human form.

"I had an interior designer come in and do it all in a couple of weeks," said Drummond.

"Was he expensive?" Bovey asked.

"She," replied Drummond. "Eight thousand pounds," he said. He looked at the briefcase in Bovey's grip. "Why don't we get down to business? I see you've come prepared."

Bovey forced a smile across his face. Drummond turned away, stepped the ten feet distance to a door, opened it and led him into the lounge. The room was dominated by a huge L shaped white leather settee beside an oak topped coffee table in the centre. The ubiquitous large screen TV screen was erected on the wall on one side, with a bricked fireplace on the other. A rich multi covered Persian rug covered the parquet floor. The sunlight was free to rain in through the French doors that led onto the patio and into the back garden.

"Please take a seat," said Drummond. Bovey sat at the end of the long settee facing the TV screen. Drummond took the single armchair at the end of the coffee table, so they were sat close to each other at an angle.

Bovey said, "may I," and gestured to put the briefcase down onto the table that doubled as a magazine drop and a footstool.

"Sure," said Drummond. "Make yourself at home. Can I get you something to drink?" he asked. "A class of wine, maybe?"

Bovey rested the briefcase flat on the table. "Maybe in a minute. I've got some paperwork for you to complete. If you don't mind, then perhaps we can celebrate with a glass of wine."

"Sure thing," said Drummond.

With that Bovey opened the lid of the briefcase and extracted a plain manila folder, which contained several pieces of paper. He opened it and took out a document. He made eye contact with Drummond.

"This is the *Memorandum of Intent* I told you about. Basically, it records your desire to create a charity. If you could read it, sign and date it, I'd be most grateful." He gave the sheet to Drummond.

It was headed, 'Memorandum of Intent'. The content basically said it was Drummond's intention to set up a charity. Drummond read the text which was relatively straight forward and didn't contain many words he didn't understand. At the bottom of the sheet was a box where he was required to put his signature, print his name, and date the document.

"That seems in order," he said. Bovey already had a fancy silver stemmed pen in his hand which he passed to Drummond. He signed the document, then printed his name and dated it. Once complete, he slipped the paper back along the table to Bovey. Drummond noticed the gold wedding band on his ring finger. Bovey glanced at the sheet fleetingly before slipping it into the manila folder.

Drummond sat back in the armchair and crossed his legs. "Tell me Michael. Are you married?" he asked.

"Yes. I've been married to Helen for what is it…." He tilted his eyes up to look at the ceiling as if the number of years he had been married to Helen was stencilled across the plaster. "Three years."

"Any children?"

"Not yet. It's a bit too early for that. How about yourself?"

"No. Not married. Looking for the lucky lady but nothing sorted yet."

Bovey smiled. He had a nice smile. His eyes were his best feature. Drummond bet that he had a nice bedside manner.

"Can I ask you about the financial arrangements?" Bovey asked in a hesitant manner.

"The cheque?"

"Yes, the cheque."

"I have it here," said Drummond. He leaned forward to the table and opened a wide, narrow drawer concealed in the end. He pulled out a single sheet of paper.

"This is a cheque for half a million pounds made payable to Michael Bovey," he said.

He placed it into Bovey's outstretched hand. A faint smile came over Bovey's lips.

"That's excellent. Once I have completed the paperwork from the charity commission I shall transfer the money from my account into the trust account and you will then be able to get the trustees on board and begin the quest to help the future sports stars of the community. A very noble cause," he said. "Oh, can I ask about my fee for setting it up?" He looked slightly stressed, as if he was embarrassed to mention it.

"What if I write you another cheque for the fee. I'll do it shortly," said Drummond.

"That's fine," said Bovey. He slipped the cheque for five hundred thousand into the folder.

"Tell me," said Drummond. "I trust that all this is hush-hush?"

Bovey looked marginally ill-at-ease. "Yes it's all confidential. Nothing has been disclosed to anyone. We are the only people who know about your plans."

Drummond smiled. He let out a sigh then a strained chuckle. "Good," he said, then he pushed himself forward to get out of the armchair. "How about that drink?" he asked.

The moment of tension was pricked.

"Yes fine. I'm driving but a small glass of wine wouldn't go amiss."

"No. Just one," said Drummond. "Why don't I show you the rest of the house," he added. Bovey didn't look as if he was too keen on the idea. Drummond saw his reluctance. "I've got some fine wine in the games room. Maybe I can challenge you to a game of pool. Do you play?" he asked.

"Not for a number of years," replied Bovey.

"One game and a glass of wine," Drummond encouraged.

Bovey relented. You could see that he wasn't mad keen on the idea. But he had to play the part of the guest in his client's home.

Drummond took him back into the reception area, across the floor and into the games room at the front of the house. The interior was plastered with large posters of famous sports stars in glass frames on the walls. The pool table was in the centre of the room. A pair of cues were laid on the baize. The blinds over the windows were down. The two arcade machines were set along one side. In the corner was a fridge unit containing a wide assortment of bottles and cans.

"You set up the balls," said Drummond. "I'll pour us a couple of drinks. White or red?"

"Do you have a Rose?"

Trust him to the fussy, thought Drummond. "No problem," he replied.

He opened the cold unit door and took out a chilled bottle of Rose wine. A relatively cheap brand he had purchased from the local supermarket.

Bovey set up the balls on the table using the triangle. At least he knew how to do that. "All set," he announced.

Drummond handed him a glass containing the wine. "You break. Your honour."

Bovey put the glass down, took one of the cues and bent down over the table to make the break. He hit the balls, hammering the cue ball into the pack. They made the solid clicking sound as they parted and spread far and wide over the blue baize.

"Good break," said Drummond. He got set over the table, took aim but screwed a simple red wide of a middle pocket.

"Hard luck," said Bovey. Hard luck my arse, thought Drummond. He moved to a side as Bovey leaned over the table and jabbed the tip of the cue onto the white ball. As the ball moved across the baize Drummond lifted the thick end of his cue over Bovey's head and brought it crashing down onto his skull.

CHAPTER 7

Outside it was wet, windy, and stormy. I dare not look out of the window at the rain beating on the glass. Behind the curtain it was darker than coal.

I had just settled down at seven-thirty to watch Coronation Street, the only soap I watch on television and follow with any interest. Carol was in the bath. I was feeling tired after my day at work. I didn't want to be disturbed this evening. I was half thinking about calling up to Carol to ask her if she wanted her back scrubbing when my mobile phone sprang into life. I instantly recognised the number in the window. It was Ray Drummond. I thought about turning the phone off, but my sense of loyalty to him made me answer the call.

"Hello." No response. "Hello," I repeated, this time in a louder tone.

"It's Ray," he said. His voice was weak and didn't carry any weight, almost as if he was depressed, fatigued or just drunk.

"Hi Ray," I said.

"He's here," Drummond said in a partial whisper.

"Who's here?" I asked. Unaware of who he was talking about.

"Bovey."

"Where?"

"In my house."

I shuddered. "What's he doing in your house?" I asked.

"Not a lot," he replied, then let out a madman's chuckle.

I closed my eyes and wished this wasn't happening. I tried to remain calm and in control of my thoughts and emotions. "Where is he?" I asked.

"In the basement."

"What's he doing in the basement?" I asked. I had been to Ray's home on several occasions. In fact, I had helped him to move in. I knew there was nothing in the basement at that time other than a few battered tea chests, so unless he had converted it into a liveable space then there had to be some ulterior motive why he had Bovey in the cellar.

"I've got him down there," he said.

"Oh Ray. For fuck sake! What have you done?" I asked.

"He must have thought I was a right cunt."

"What are you on about?"

"Asking me for the money. Asking me to write him a personal cheque for half a million pounds. He must have assumed he could roll all over me."

"Ray, I haven't got a clue what you're talking about," I said.

Drummond let out a kind of whimper as if he had just realised that he had done something he shouldn't have done, but it was too late to turn the clock back.

"I need help," he pleaded. "Please get here."

I didn't want to get involved. That was the last thing on my mind, but something told me I had to. "Is Bovey okay?" I asked.

"I hit him with a pool cue," he replied.

I paused for a long moment wondering what the hell I could say to that. It came to my lips. "Is he hurt?" I asked.

"Yeah. I think so."

"Think so?" I exclaimed. "Oh, Ray for God's sake." I wanted to end the call at this point but if there was a chance that I could do something to prevent a tragedy then I had to try. "Wait there. I'll be right around," I said and ended the call.

I grabbed my coat and my cars keys. As I got to the bottom of the stairs I called up to Carol. "I've got to go out." I said in a raised voice. "Urgent business." Either, she didn't hear me above the sound of the splashing water or if she did she choose to ignore me. I went out into the cold night and got into my car. I was shaking with fear at what I might discover at Drummonds.

Thankfully the roads were quiet. The inclement weather had seen to that. It took me a little over fifteen minutes to drive the five miles to the posh side of the town. I was half expecting to find a police car and an ambulance outside of the house. When I arrived, there was no evidence of any activity outside. Very few people were around at eight o'clock on a cold, dank November night. Outside of the house I could see Drummond's BMW parked on the forecourt. A single security light over the front door was on. There were lights burning in the games room and in one of the upstairs front bedrooms.

I decided to drive passed the house rather than go through the open gate and park in the forecourt. I was thinking on my feet. I drove on for about one hundred yards, then stopped opposite one of the other big houses on the road and killed the engine. I glanced along to check the pavement ahead to see if anyone was around. When I was certain no body was near I turned the lights off and got out of the car. It was with a great deal of care that I closed the door. I didn't want to alert anyone that I was here. Hopefully, there weren't many curtain *twitchers* in this neighbourhood. That and most of the houses were set back gave me a feeling that I might be lucky on that score.

  I ventured along the path and dipped my hands into the pocket of my jacket and attempted to bury my head into the high collar. Within a second or two I was at the front of the house. I briskly walked through the metal gate, across the brick forecourt and towards the front door.

  Drummond opened the door as soon as I knocked. The face that appeared in the opening was anxious and shiny with sweat. He looked at me and gave me a nervy smile.

  "Where is he?" I asked.

  "In the basement."

  I didn't ask him for permission to enter the house. I walked into the reception area and to the door that led down to the cellar. As I opened the door a wave of cold, fusty air hit me. I turned the overhead light on and descended the dozen concrete steps. Despite the total floor space of the house the basement was only a small space, about fifteen feet square at a guess. It had a bare stone floor and plastered walls. The overhead light was dim, but I could see that

Bovey was laid face down on the floor. I could also see that the back of his head was matted with blood. Lots of blood.

"How long as he been here?" I asked.

"A few hours."

"How many times did you hit him?"

"Once or twice."

"Well was it one or two?"

"Maybe three."

I looked at Drummond and wished I had never seen him before.

"Is he dead?" he asked.

"I don't know."

I had recently completed a First Aid course at my place of employment, so I knew the basics. I took his left side shoulder and managed to turn him over onto his back. Despite the light I could see that his eyes were closed. Once he was on his back I took his left hand, placed it across his chest and put it by his chin, then I raised his left leg at the knee. Once he was in position I managed to roll him ninety degrees to put him onto his side and into a recovery position. All the time Drummond was watching me. He didn't say a word.

"Get a blanket," I demanded. "And call for an ambulance."

"No police," he said firmly and defiantly.

I relented. "Okay. But at least get him a blanket for God's sake. He's going to freeze to death."

Miraculously, Drummond ceded to my request. He went up the steps and out of the basement. My initial reaction was to cry then run out, but I didn't. My first aid training kicked in. I got down on my knees, put my head close to him and got my ear against his mouth. I thought I could hear him trying to breath. His lips moved or maybe I imagined it. His breath sounded shallow. He looked pale but maybe that was the light. I felt his neck to feel for a pulse around his carotid artery. I thought I felt a pulse. It was very weak. He was alive but barely hanging on. I took out my mobile phone and turned it on. The reception bars were non-existent. I couldn't ring out from here.

Then I heard Drummond coming down the stairs. He had a bed blanket in his hand. He saw me with the phone in my hand. "What you doing?" he barked.

"We need to get him into hospital," I said.

"I told you *no* police," he snapped.

I didn't reply. I yanked the blanket out of his hand and spread it over Bovey. Then I wondered how Drummond had got him down the stairs. Suffice to say it was a question I didn't ask him. There were a whole series of questions I wanted to ask him. Why? What? How? When? What now? But now wasn't the time.

It was at this juncture that I decided to try and talk some sense into Drummond. What I didn't want was him around Bovey. I made the decision to take Drummond upstairs and get him sat down in the lounge. Maybe, I could persuade him to call for medical attention for Bovey, or maybe I could use the landline phone to do it myself.

"Let's go up," I suggested.

"Where?"

"Upstairs. Into the lounge."

He paused for a moment as though he suspected I was going to try something underhand. "Okay," he said somewhat reluctantly.

Bovey was still alive but maybe for not much longer. We ascended the stairs and stepped back into the reception. He led the way into the lounge. We sat around the table. I looked at Drummond and he looked at me. As I looked at him I recalled what he had said about giving me the deeds to the house if I helped him.

"What were you saying on the phone about a cheque for half a million?" I asked.

He told me in a very matter-of-fact and level-headed way about how he had contacted Bovey with the idea of setting up a charity and how he was going to donate half a million pounds. He told me everything. How Bovey had asked him to make out a cheque to him for that amount and how he was going to transfer it into the charity account when it was up and running. I must admit that I did find it a rather peculiar way of doing business. Maybe it was legitimate. Or maybe Ray was right, Bovey was trying to scam him.

"How did he get here?" I asked.

"In a car."

"Where is it?"

"In the garage."

"You can't leave it here."

It was at this point that I noticed the briefcase on the table.

"Who's that?" I asked.

"His."

I carefully opened the lid and extracted the manila folder. I hardly dare touch it.

"What's in this?" I asked.

"Something called a *Memorandum of Intent* and the cheque."

"Where's your copy?"

"Of what?"

"This memorandum."

"He never gave me one."

I considered this strange. Then I looked at the cheque. Sure, enough it was a cheque made out to Michael Bovey for half a million pounds. Not to his firm of accountants or to the name of a charity. It was made out to him. What I would do with five thousand pounds, let alone half a million, I thought. I looked at the memorandum.

"This looks iffy to me. I doubt it has any legal integrity or significance," I said.

What it did have was Drummond's signature as did the cheque. I seriously began to wonder if all this was bullshit. Maybe he was trying to pull the wool over Drummond's eyes after all. I didn't know.

I advised him to burn the memorandum and the cheque. The next thing I said even took me by surprise. "We've got to get rid of his car and his briefcase."

Drummond looked at me sharply. His face was serious.

"Yeah, you're right. Your always right. You've always been straight with me," he said.

He was like a little kid who wanted a bigger kid to look after him in the playground. He clearly hadn't thought this through in a rational manner. It was all on impulse. Or if he had, he was playing a very dangerous game.

"Who knows he was coming here?" I asked.

Drummond ran the tip of his tongue between his lips. "As far as I know. No one."

"Who knows that you were setting up this charity and he was doing it for you?" I asked.

"As far as I know no one. I asked him not to say anything to anyone and he said he wouldn't."

I took in all this information and filtered it through my mind. If we were going to get away with this I needed to think straight.

"If that's the case and he kept to his word, then we might just get away with it," I said.

"Do you think?" he asked.

"If we're canny. Maybe."

I thought of the next course of action.

"Right the first thing we need to do is to get rid of his car. You can't leave it in your garage. You drive his. I'll take mine. You follow me to Tinkers Wood. We'll leave it there by those picnic tables. Do you know where I mean?"

"Yeah. I've been there before."

Tinkers Wood was a lover's lane with several off-road tracks leading deep into a wood that was a good ten to twenty acres in size. There was a small tarmacked area adjacent to a few picnic tables. On a night like this in the middle of autumn there wouldn't be anyone around for miles. I had a secondary thought.

"You take the city route," I said. "I'll go around the other way. We'll meet there. Ensure you wear a hat and try to keep your face covered. Wear a pair of sunglasses if you have to."

"Do you think?" Drummond asked.

"No, I'm only joking. We'll look after him when we get back." I didn't know how I had the nerve to joke at a time like this. I was getting in too deep. I was getting involved. Something in the back of my mind told me I was an idiot. That I was committing suicide. That it would all end in tears. It was too late. I was determined to get money or the house or both. At this moment in time my marriage was as rocky as a paddle steamer in a force nine gale. My job was as rewarding as a kick in the family jewels. I had an opportunity here and as much as I would hate myself in the morning it was one I was going to take.

I asked him for a pair of gloves. He went into the kitchen and came back with a pair of oven gloves which I slipped over my hands. I opened the briefcase lid and looked through the papers.

"What're doing?" he asked.

"Looking to see if there's anything that links him to you."

"Good idea," he said.

There were some official looking papers. A writing pad with some scribbles on a single sheet. There was nothing that looked as if it could connect him to Drummond.

"Okay. We'll take this and leave it in his car." I sighed aloud. "Okay, let's do it."

"How about him?" he asked.

I had nearly forgotten about Bovey. It had been ten minutes since we had come up here.

"Let's go and see," I suggested.

We went down to the basement. He wasn't moving at all. I got down on my knees and put my ear to his mouth. There was no sound. He looked grey. I felt the vein in his neck. There was no pulse. The back of his head was covered with blood that was matted in his hair. I got onto my knees and looked up at Drummond.

"He's dead." I announced. I looked at my watch. The time was eight forty-five.

CHAPTER 8

Drummond drove Bovey's Lexus saloon car out of the garage. I walked the one hundred yards further up the path to my car. As I got into my car Drummond was easing out of the forecourt and onto the lane.

As I started my car and moved away I looked into the rear-view mirror and deep into my eyes. This was going to end well, or it was going to end badly. I was determined to ensure that it ended okay for me. It was going to cost Drummond his house and some.

I took the long way around to Tinkers Wood along the ring road that encircled the town. The rain had ceased, but it was blowing a gale which was whipping up the fallen leaves on the road and depositing them on the windscreen. Several got caught under the windscreen wipers.

It took me twenty minutes to get to the rendezvous. It was as dark as hell out here in Tinkers. It would have made a great location for some creepy slasher movie. The car park was empty of vehicles and people. There was one car parked by the picnic tables. It was Drummond in Bovey's Lexus. The lights were out.

I parked parallel to the car but kept at least ten yards distance between me and him. As I stopped Drummond got out and quickly made his way to me. He opened the door.

"Where's the briefcase?" I asked.

"On the passenger seat."

I advised him to go back and empty the contents over the front seats and to leave the doors open but to ensure he kept the keys. After all a car-jacker or a joy rider was hardly likely to worry if the doors were left open or the keys had been taken. The discarded papers would suggest that someone had stolen the car then found the case and rifled through it.

Drummond did as I suggested while I stayed in my car and observed him. I watched him empty the contents of the briefcase over the front seats A minute later he was in my car and we were heading back into town along the main road.

Drummond asked me what we should do with him. I said I didn't know. Let me think about it. I suggested we leave it for a couple of days at least. Bovey's wife and work colleagues would soon realise that he had gone missing. When the police found his car and the papers strung over the seats they would rank it up a notch. If no one knew that he was going to see Drummond, then there was no connection between them. We had to think. We had to manage this. I related this to Drummond. He agreed.

I dropped him off on the edge of the estate where he lived. I advised him not to contact me by telephone, email or by any other method, including carrier pigeon and drums.

I told him I would come around to his house in two days. He agreed to this. In the meantime, I advised him to visit a local DIY store or a garden centre to purchase a couple of large, hard-wearing plastic sheets, two pairs of disposal overalls with hoods, two pairs of gardening gloves, some duct tape, two pairs of boot covers and a Stanley knife. He didn't ask me why. I told him not to purchase them with a credit or debit card but to pay cash. If anyone asked him why he needed them he had to say he was doing some gardening or something on those lines.

I arrived home at nine-thirty. Carol asked me where I had been. I said I had gone for a drive because I needed some fresh air. She didn't speak to me again until the following morning.

The next day I went to work as normal, getting there for nine o'clock. Thankfully it was Friday. We didn't do a lot on Friday. The office tended to close at around four o'clock. If the bosses were away on a shindig we usually got away at around three-thirty. I stayed on to four o'clock then I met Carol in town as we usually visited a supermarket to get in the food and supplies for the weekend. We went in together and did the shopping just like any other couple.

It was in the car going back to the council estate where we lived when the local news came on the radio. Police in the town were looking for the local businessman and accountant, Michael Bovey, whose Lexus car had been found abandoned in Tinkers Wood. If anyone knew his whereabouts, then they were asked to contact the local police or his office. I gulped hard. Carol asked me how work had gone today. I said, 'same-old, same-old.'

We had tea then settled down to watch TV and generally chill. I prayed that Drummond wouldn't try to contact me. I turned off my mobile and dare not turn my computer on to check my email or Twitter page.

CHAPTER 9

The following morning, I was up at eight forty-five. I put the radio on and listened to the local news. The main story concerned the storm the other evening and the cost of the damage it had caused to a local school. Part of the roof had been blown off and had fallen onto a bike shed and some other out-buildings. The next story concerned a local football team who were playing a game in the first round of the FA Cup for the first time in their history. Then the next news item. Police were still searching for local accountant Michael Bovey, who hadn't been seen since he left his office at midday on Thursday. The police were becoming increasingly concerned for his safety.

I knew it would only be a matter of time before his picture appeared in the local newspaper then on the local news. Then I thought of Tony Plummer, the man I had advised Drummond to contact for information about Helen Bovey. If Drummond had mentioned my name and Plummer had heard the request for information, then I might be getting a knock from the police any day soon. I felt a sudden bolt of angst in the pit of my stomach and I was bitten by an anxiety attack. I suddenly felt ill and the urge to vomit.

I decided, rightly or wrongly to contact Plummer to ask him if he had heard the story about Michael Bovey. It was with a great deal of trepidation that I picked up the telephone. I came up with a story about how a friend had asked me how he could find out where an old flame was living. How I had given him his name, but the friend hadn't told me the name of the person he was trying to find. Anyway, was he able to help? If he said it was Helen Bovey, then I would say something on the lines of what a coincidence. Aren't the police looking for a Michael Bovey? Are they related by any chance? I rang Tony Plummer's home. The telephone was answered by a girl who said she was his daughter. The next thing she said gladdened my heart. Her mother and father had gone away to Spain for a few weeks and wouldn't be back in the country for another ten days. I blew out a massive sigh of relief. My heartbeat went back to something approaching normal. I thanked her and put down the phone. I had some grace time. Time to think it through.

That day I didn't do much. At around noon we had some lunch then both Carol and I took Jasper for a walk on the common. It was a lovely day. The leaves on the trees, well those that remained on the branches, were now a banana skin shade of yellow. The grass was moist, and the smell of dew was strong. We walked arm-in-arm. I threw a hard sponge ball for Jasper to scamper off across the field to retrieve. He seemed a lot more interested in the other dogs. He was part-trained so my call soon had him back on the trail of the ball. We loved Jasper, he was like our baby boy. Maybe if I got Drummond's house as promised, sold it and moved into a new house with money in the bank then we would start a family of our own.

Things took an incredible twist at six o'clock in the evening. After the main UK and international news on TV, the local bulletin came on. As I had predicted the disappearance of Michael Bovey had crept to the top of the pile, above the usual mundane items. However, the turn of events, caught me by complete surprise. I had never envisaged this, not in a million years. I listened to the news report with slack jawed incredulity. A local reporter who looked to be standing on a lane in front of Bovey's home said the police were now saying that Michael Bovey may have faked his own disappearance. In the last couple of hours, the police had revealed that Bovey was being investigated by them following a number of complaints from several of his clients that he had embezzled them, or in plainer words, stolen money from them. The police were talking in terms of several hundreds of thousands of pounds which had gone missing from their accounts which Bovey had access to. Plod were working on the assumption that he was aware of their investigation and that on learning this he had done a runner before the police came to arrest him. The camera then panned away from the face of the reporter to focus on the front of his house, then back to the reporter.

"Geez," I said under my breath, but loud enough for Carol to hear me.

"What?" she asked.

"This bloke may have been stealing money from his clients. Look at that house. Why did he have to do that?" I asked.

Carol said something very profound. That his house didn't mean to say he had money. He could have been in debt up to his eyeballs. What was the mortgage on a place like that? She asked.

Of course, she was right. Just because he was an accountant and lived in a big house didn't mean that he was minted. It may have been a cover. All the time he had his fingers in the till stealing from those who trusted him.

The reporter finished by saying that the local police had informed their colleagues all over the country and that the Border Agency were on the lookout for Michael Bovey, who may attempt to leave the country on a false passport. Gordon Bennett, I said. This was a local sensation. It completely blew my socks off. There was also a subtle reference to suicide. Maybe he had taken his own life as police were searching Tinkers Wood, the place where he had left his car. The reporter said that his wife and other members of the family were not prepared to make a statement at this time. If he was by any chance watching this programme, then they begged him to come home.

As the reporter concluded the report and the news went to the local sports news Carol took the remote control off me and turned the channel over. I never uttered a word. I was too relieved and happy to receive the news that Bovey was an alleged thief. Drummond was right all along, Bovey was trying to stitch him up. Whilst that didn't make what Drummond did any more palatable, it made me feel better in myself.

CHAPTER 10

The following morning, Sunday, I was up at around nine. I made Carol breakfast and took it up to her. She was working a new shift pattern at work starting from today. Her rota for the next six days was the four in the afternoon to ten at night shift. I would take her to the store at about three-thirty then return to pick her up at ten this evening.

For the remainder of the morning I just potted around the house. The morning had begun overcast. By noon it was sunny and bright, though cool for this time of the year. There was hardly a cloud in the sky. Jasper was becoming restless. A good excuse for me to get out of the house. Sunday was a good day to get the body out of Drummond's house. Nothing much happened around here on a Sunday. For most of yesterday and last night I had been thinking about how we were going to get the corpse out of the house, then an idea came to me. It wasn't the most brilliant idea I'd ever had, but it was all I could think of. I had to run it by Drummond. There was no way on this earth that I was going to do it on the landline or my mobile.

I put on my jacket and a pair of wellington boots. On seeing me getting ready, Jasper went crazy. He knew when it was time for walkies. His tail wagged. Carol was in the kitchen preparing Sunday lunch. I put my head around the door. "Just taking Jasper, I'll be about an hour," I said.

Off we went towards the common. I passed one of our neighbours, tending to his garden. I stopped to chat to him for a minute.

As I got to the end of our road, I turned left and headed to some local shops where there was a pay-phone telephone box.

I went in and called Drummond on his mobile. He was pleased to hear from me. You could hear it in his voice. Our conversation was brief. I told him to listen and not to interrupt. I wanted to see him at eight o'clock tonight. We had to move the problem and I knew a good place. When he asked me where? I replied a place we both know well. I asked him if he had the special equipment. He said he had got the stuff. We were almost talking in a coded, secret language. Neither of us wanted to mention the body. My last instruction to him was that he had to pick me up from the petrol station adjacent to the shopping centre car park at eight o'clock sharp. He said sure.

On returning home, Carol had made lunch which consisted of sandwiches and beer. She made a mean corn beef, tomato, and lettuce combination. It was my favourite. She really looked after me. She was far too good for an arse like me. Our clear the air talk had been the tonic in our relationship. Though I may not always display it, I loved her like crazy. We had been married for four years. She was the best thing to ever happen to me. That is why I was helping Drummond. I wanted her to have the best she could have. She deserved it. We had talked about starting a family, but we were still paying out too much on the mortgage for this place, and though my job was okay I never earned a lot. If I made twenty thousand last year than I had done well. If, and it was a big if, Drummond was true to his word and gave me the deeds to his house then we could start to think about having that baby. Carol would make a great mother. Actually, I wouldn't make a bad dad.

That day, Carol and I left our home at three-thirty. I drove the five miles to the supermarket, parked in the car park and walked her into the store. It was heaving with people. I left her at the staff entrance, then went inside the store to purchase a few items we needed. After that I returned home and watched some sport on television. I had one eye on the clock and one on the TV. I was thinking about later and the gruesome task of moving the body from out of the basement and what we had to do to ensure we didn't leave anything behind. On a cold, damp Sunday night in the last week of November, Tinkers Wood should be deserted. There was a spot on the edge of the wood where we could leave the body in deep shrub and hope it stayed hidden there for ever.

It was seven-thirty when I left home and drove back to the shopping centre. Jasper was by my side. He seemed a little peeved that I was taking him out at this time of the night and into the cold night air. He looked at me with his hound-dog eyes as if to say, *'what the fuck are you up to?'* Woe betide if she finds out. I told him to mind his own business. I wanted to stay focused. It was a case of hoping that Drummond would be the same.

Once we were in the supermarket car-park I parked fairly close to the store entrance, but I had no intention of going inside. Instead, I walked towards the exit and made my way to the petrol station at the edge of the car-park, using Jasper's need to go to toilet as a reason for coming this way.

I stood by some bushes just across the way from the turn-in to the petrol station and waited for Jasper to do a number and for Drummond to arrive. The night was starry, overhead a million stars twinkled. I could just make out the roar of an airliner over head. I wondered where it was going. Somewhere better than this place. I waited for Drummond. Needless to say, he wasn't on time. I cursed the useless twat. I was sticking my neck out for him. I questioned myself why I was doing this, but I never got an adequate answer.

It was ten past eight when I spotted his BMW. He missed me and went into the car park and parked in a spot about fifty yards away. As it was the car park was hardly full. The supermarket was the only shop open this late on a Sunday night. The lights and the huge neon sign were blazing out from the front.

I walked the fifty yards to the car. "Your late," I snapped as I opened the door and climbed in.

"Sorry. Got lost."

"Got lost! Are you ready to do this?" I asked.

"Sure." He appeared to be amazingly laid back.

"Well then let's go."

Jasper lay on the rug spread across the back seat.

We arrived on the estate where Drummond lived ten minutes after leaving the car park. As he we approached the lane where his house was located I slid down the front seat in order to get out of view. Once he had driven onto the forecourt in front of his house he activated the roller shutter door at the garage, then edged the car inside. His SUV was at the other side adjacent to the door that lead into the house.

Once the roller shutter was closed we got out of the BMW and entered the house. I looked at my watch. It was already half past eight.

"Okay, let's get a move on. I don't want to stay here longer than I have to," I said.

We went into the reception area by the front door. On the floor, there were a pair of disposable overalls, gloves, and shoe covers, parcel tape and a Stanley knife. He had got parcel tape rather than duct tape. He said it was going to be much better for the job in hand. I didn't question him.

Before getting down to it I took Jasper back into the garage and put him on the front seat of the SUV. "Sorry fella," I said. "I won't be long." He yawned, then lay down on the seat. What a trooper, I thought.

Once I was back in the reception area we got down to the task with business like concentration. Thankfully, Drummond was just as focused as me. We slipped the overalls on over our jeans and t-shirts, then the gloves and the shoe covers. The overalls had hoods which we put over our heads, then zipped them up tight.

"Where are the plastic sheets?" I asked.

Drummond said they were in the basement. Once we were dressed we went to the door, collected the other items, and descended down the stairs to the cellar. There was a horrible fusty smell of trapped dusty air and death. The naked bulb hanging from the ceiling was hardly strong enough to illuminate the dark corners. It sent a shudder down my spine. The cold air went straight through the thin cotton like material. We approached the body. Bovey was in the same position I had left him. I carefully removed the blanket and put it to a side. Drummond opened the plastic sheet and spread it out fully on the floor adjacent to the body. Once the sheet was spread out we both moved around to the back of the body and got down on our knees. Between us were able to roll Bovey's stiff cold corpse onto the sheet. It wasn't easy work. I felt a field of sweat beads on my forehead.

"You'll need to give this floor a decent wash. Get rid of anything we leave," I said.

"Sure," he replied.

"Never mind *sure*," I snapped. "Make absolutely one hundred percent certain you do it. It could prevent us going to jail."

Drummond didn't reply. Between us we managed to get the body onto the sheet. Once he was on we simply wrapped the sheet around him. Like you would wrap a joint of beef in tinfoil. I used the knife to cut off several lengths of the parcel tape which we used to secure the ends. Within a couple of minutes, we had managed to almost mummify him in the sheet. We had nearly used a full roll of tape to secure the bag.

Once it was tight I took his legs, Drummond took his shoulders. Working as a team we were able to carry the body up the stone steps out of the basement and lay him on the reception room floor. We took a minutes breather. I looked at this incongruous sight in front of me. A once breathing, living human being who was now wrapped in a plastic sheet. His face was pressing at the transparent cover. It was a horrific sight. He didn't deserve this. What in God's name was I doing helping to dispose of a body? This could land me in prison for many, many years. Too late. I had done it. It was all my idea.

"Come on," said Drummond in an encouraging manner. "Into the garage." He took Bovey's feet. I took his shoulders and got a good grip of the sheet. We carried the body across the floor to the door that led into the garage. As we passed the bottom of the stairs the light cascading in through the window on the landing reflected in the plastic coating. Drummond said something which I didn't catch. I didn't ask him to repeat it. I was knackered. All the time I was conscious that I hadn't to leave any of my DNA or anything else on the bag.

We managed to get him through the door and into the garage. The tailgate of the SUV was up. We succeeded in getting the corpse into the back of the vehicle in no time. Jasper looked to me with a questioning look in his eyes. He knew I was acting strange, but then he averted his eyes and looked straight ahead, as if he was saying this was nothing to do with him.

Once Drummond had locked the door leading into the house, I climbed into the back of the SUV and lay next to the body. Drummond activated the garage door. Once the metal roller was all the way up he got into the driver's seat, started the engine and drove out into the night. I stayed down well below the window level.

We were heading to a spot close to the fringe of Tinkers Wood to dispose of the body.

CHAPTER 11

The traffic was light. It was a Sunday night. Tomorrow was a work day for many and a school day for kids. People were content to stay in; anyway, there wasn't much to do on a cold night, though the sky was clear it was bitterly cold. The weather men were predicting a frosty start to Monday. By the temperature reading on the SUV dashboard they weren't going to be wrong. There was a thin white vale of frosty mist in the air right now.

We approached Tinkers Wood on the circular road that went all the around the wood. The locals called it, 'Round Tinkers Lane'. It was tarmacked for much of the way then it became nothing much more than a dirt road for a few hundred yards. The track led to a one-story derelict building. Further along from that was a disused water treatment plant behind a barbwire topped metal fence.

We soon passed the entrance to the car park where we had left Bovey's car. I instructed Drummond to go further around and take the dirt road that led to the old Water Works. Up front Jasper was sitting on the passenger seat as good as gold. Drummond would even pat him on the head from time to time.

After about a quarter of a mile further along the road the tarmac became a dirt track full of water filled potholes and wet, slippery mud.

"Once we get near to the derelict house pull up. We'll put him in the undergrowth," I instructed.

"Sure thing," was Drummond's response. The uneven terrain soon had the SUV rocking from side to side. Within a matter of twenty seconds of him saying, 'sure thing', he pulled up. I looked up and out of the window There was nothing out there but an impenetrable dark. There was no evidence of anyone around.

"Okay let's do it," I said.

Drummond got out of the driver's door and came around to the back and opened the tailgate. I slipped out beside the plastic bag and got to my feet. My feet were wrapped in the foot covers.

Between us we pulled the plastic bag along the floor. Drummond took the end where his head was. I had the feet. Between us we carried Bovey's body towards the wood.

We had to negotiate a low, two-row wooden fence. Once we had got over the obstacle we carried the body into the wood. We literally trampled through bramble bushes and various shrubs. I nearly lost my balance on a couple of occasions. It was too eerie for words. The wind got up and blew in the treetops to send a shower of rain drops cascading over us. It was no picnic.

In some places the bushes were quite thick and snagged on my overall. Almost to the point where it ripped open. I didn't know what kind of bushes and shrubs they were, just that they were thick. The moonlight shining through the trees caught us in its bright spotlight. What an incongruous sight. Two men dressed in 'Noddy' suits carrying a large plastic bag into the undergrowth. Not an everyday sight. It was in a word: ghoulish.

There were all kinds of weird sounds. We had to dodge around the thicker shrubs and step carefully. The ground was wet and subsequently spongy in places. When we were about one hundred yards from the back of the derelict house deep into the wood I stopped. "There's no need to go any further," I whispered.

"Okay," said Drummond.

We laid the body on the ground, hiding it as best as we could by attempting to roll it under a shrub of some description. In truth we were both out on our feet. To continue would have been silly. We had taken him as far as we could go. This spot had to make do.

"Let's go," I encouraged.

Without a word passing between us we trampled along the path we had made and went back to the SUV.

Before I got into the vehicle, I slipped the overall and the foot covers off and threw them into the storage area, then I climbed into the front passenger seat next to Jasper. I kept the gloves on. Jasper was so pleased to see me he licked my face.

On the way back into town I advised Drummond to get the car washed and valeted but to leave it for a few days at least. Also, to burn his overall and the shoe covers and to get rid of the tape, the knife and so forth. We didn't want to leave any clues that could be used as evidence. I also reiterated that he had to get rid of the Memorandum and the cheque by burning them. He said 'sure'.

We arrived back in the shopping centre car park at a quarter to ten. Just in time for Carol leaving work. I retrieved the overall I had been wearing and the boot covers.

Before leaving I suggested to Drummond that we lie low for the next few days. I would contact him in three days from now, then perhaps we could meet to discuss other matters. He said 'sure'.

I took the overall and boot covers and walked Jasper to my car. Once there I placed the overall, gloves and foot covers into the boot and stuffed them under Jasper's blanket.

I watched Drummond drive out of the car park. What a liability, I thought. That guy was going to get me sent to prison for a long time. Why did I ever have to meet him? Too late. The deed was done.

Once I was in sitting in the driver's seat I checked my mobile phone for any missed messages. There were none.

Carol finished work at ten; we were home for twenty past the hour.

CHAPTER 12

Sixty hours went by. It was now Wednesday. There was nothing much to report. On that day, I got home from work at just after five-thirty. For a change, I had had a decent day. They were making some personnel changes. My boss for whom I had little regard was rumoured to be moving on. Things were looking up. However, my mind was dominated by the need to get things sorted out with Drummond. He had promised me his house in exchange for my help. Now he had to deliver on that promise.

Carol had gone to work at three-thirty, leaving some food in the oven. All I had to do was to turn it on. First, I turned on the radio for the local news. Bombshell. I couldn't believe what I heard. It was like a bad dream. The newsreader said that in the past two hours a body had been found on the edge of Tinkers Wood, wrapped in a plastic sheet.

Apparently, someone walking a dog had let the animal off the lead. The dog had followed his nose and found the body deep in the undergrowth. I cursed like mad. This wasn't supposed to happen. How on earth had someone found it so soon? It was far too early to say who it was or the likely cause of death. I felt sick. I went to the sink bowl and nearly threw up.

This changed things big time. I wondered how long it would be before the police did some more investigating and came up with leads? They were not stupid. I was hoping that the body would have laid there throughout the winter months; needless to say, I was wrong. Even though the body had been found it didn't mean to say they would put Drummond in the frame. I was getting ahead of myself. I decided to carry on. Drummond was expecting me this evening. I was determined to keep the appointment.

    I left my home at seven and drove to the supermarket car park. The place was quiet for a Wednesday night. There was some big football game on television. England were playing an important international match. I might have stayed in to watch it but not tonight.

    Once I had parked the car I put Jasper on his lead. We walked the half a mile or so from the shopping centre car park to Drummond's house

    It was around eight when I got to his home. Assuming he hadn't heard the news, I didn't think it was a good idea to tell Drummond that someone had found a body in Tinkers Wood. That would have really freaked him out. Whilst the body was yet to be formally identified I knew it was Bovey. Nevertheless, I was determined to press him on the promise to give me the deeds to the house. I had stuck my neck out too far on this occasion. I wasn't going to listen to any bullshit.

    He knew that I could be nasty and aggressive if it came to it. Like the time he and I had been on a day out to the races and had come across some football fans arsing about in a Motorway Service station. We nearly had a fight with a couple of them. How we laughed about it later.

As soon as I got to Drummond's I slipped off the pavement and went to the front door. A light was on in the games room. I pressed the button in the intercom unit.

"Who is it?" Drummond asked.

"It's me. Do you fancy some waffles and beans? I'm paying." I said in a mimicking American accent.

"What?" Drummond asked.

"Just open up will you," I snapped.

The door opened. I stepped inside dragging Jasper behind me. He hated this house with a passion. He knew what had gone on inside these four walls.

Then the penny dropped. Drummond laughed out loud. "Oh right. Jackie Brown. The scene were Roby goes to collect Beaumont Livingstone to shoot him in the boot of his car."

We were both great Tarantino fans. "That's it. Great movie." I said.

"Yeah. Certainly is. Come into the lounge." Drummond said.

I left Jasper in the reception area by the door and secured his lead around the door handle. He seemed content to sit there and rest after our long walk.

Both Drummond and I stepped into the lounge. He was wearing a pair of long shorts and a simple t-shirt. The wide-screen TV was on. The England game was on. The volume was turned low. The room was pleasantly warm. I sat on the L shaped settee adjacent to his armchair. The blinds over the French doors leading onto the patio were closed. Drummond took his seat to my left and clapped his eyes on the screen.

"Who's playing?" I asked.

"England versus Spain."

"Any score?"

"One nil."

"Who to?"

"Them."

The crowd roared as Spain came close to extending their lead.

Drummond looked at me. "Drink?" he asked.

"No thanks. To be honest, I've come to talk business." I said.

"Oh right."

"Remember what you said?" He didn't reply. "That you'd give me this house for helping you."

"Sure." There he goes again. Sure this. Sure that. He was beginning to get on my nerves.

"Well that's what I've done."

"Yeah, you're right."

"I could have shopped you, but I didn't."

Drummond looked at me with a curious expression on his face. "What are you getting at?" he asked, all dumb.

"I've come to get it sorted," I said.

"And so we shall, but you didn't think I was serious. Did you?"

I was angered by his words. "Too fucking right, I did."

He looked at me with his mouth marginally open as if he hadn't calculated my reaction. He seemed surprised by my candour and aggressive attitude.

"Yeah okay. Your right. You've helped me, and I really appreciate it. I admit it, I owe you big time." He shifted his position in the seat and edged closer to the end of the table. "Are you sure you don't want that drink?" he asked.

"Yes. I'm sure," I said.

"You want the house. Right?"

"Yes."

"Okay." He was looking at the TV screen. "Oh, my word. What a goal. See that?"

My eyes went to the screen. In that split-second Drummond had pulled open a drawer in the table. I didn't know it was there. His hand went inside, and he quickly and swiftly pulled something out. It looked remarkably like a gun to me. A small handgun. In the poor light I could just see the black, grey metal and the end of the barrel. I thought it might be a fancy lighter or a toy. Maybe it was his idea of a joke, but I wasn't laughing, and neither was he.

"I'm a twat, am I?" he asked.

"What?" was my stunned response. It was like a scene from a Tarantino movie. All the great cut throat dialogue and acting.

Nevertheless, if I was going to survive this I had to act quickly. He was pointing the gun at me from about six feet or so. The trigger was lodged against his right-hand index finger.

He diverted his eyes from me for a split second. Now acting instinctively, I reacted. I shot forward across the six feet gap and grabbed his right hand. In doing so I was able to lever myself up and get to my feet. A struggle ensured with both of us trying to get firm hold of the weapon. If he came into range I could head-butt him on the nose, but he was lower than me. He managed to get to his feet. I could feel the metal and the bulk of the gun on my body as it was sandwiched between us. I knew he had been pumping iron, so he was bound to be strong, but I was getting the upper hand. I could feel the barrel of the gun turning away from me. I channelled all my strength into my hands. This had been going on for about five seconds. We were both wincing like crazy. He looked into my eyes. We had the briefest of staring competitions. I won. His face was screwed in exasperation as he tried to turn the tide. Then the gun went off with a 'kaboom'.

Even though the sound was muffled by our bodies it still rang loud in my ears. I thought I had been shot in the stomach or chest. I anticipated pain and the sensation of warm blood on my skin. The pain and the sensation never came. Drummond's face contorted into a grimace. His neck veins seemed to bulge out a mile. His eyes became as wide as saucers. His mouth was open. His grip began to reduce over a period of what felt like ten seconds but was a fraction of that.

Everything seemed to be in slow-motion. Then I was aware of the smell and taste of cordite in my mouth. He slumped back. I let go. He fell against the armchair arm rest. As his backside hit the armrest he slid onto the seat in a seated position. His hands came together as he reached for his chest. I heard Jasper cry.

Drummond's t-shirt was drenched with blood. I froze and just stared at him like a frightened rabbit in the headlights. His eyes went to me. He was making a rattling noise as though he was fighting for breath. He tried to say something, but he no longer had the energy to get it out.

"Frigging hell Ray," I said. Those were to be the last words Drummond ever heard.

His right hand dropped to his lap. The gun was still in the palm of his hand. I looked down at my front. My jacket and shirt were splattered with blood. I could feel damp on my face. I remained in a frozen like state. Like a statue. I couldn't believe what had just happened. The commentator on the TV was rambling on. Drummond seemed to lose the power to keep his head erect so it slumped to a side then he breathed his last ever breath.

My eyes, instinctively, travelled around the room. I glanced at the window and looked out through the gaps in the blind to the wall of dark beyond. Then I stepped back along the edge of the settee and away from him. A series of disconnected thoughts and feelings were percolating in my head; relief that I had survived, then horror that he was dead. Then a sense of my own self-preservation came into my head. I had to get away from here but do so without leaving a shred of evidence that I had been here. Slowly and deliberately I backed out of the room towards the door leading into the reception. I took my jacket and shirt off, then my shoes and socks. I placed them in a pile on the floor by the door. As I emerged into the reception area I heard Jasper whimper.

"Okay boy," I said.

As I knew the house even in the dark I went into straight into the kitchen. I found what I was looking for in a drawer, a plastic bag. When I came back into the reception area I put my jacket and shirt into the bag and tied it tight.

I was thinking on my feet. Next, I ascended the stairs to the upper floor. Once on the landing I went straight into a bathroom. I had to get the blood off my hands and face. On entering I had to turn the light on to see what I was doing. I looked at myself in the mirror. I didn't even recognise myself. I looked like an alien.

There was blood on my face. There was blood on my hands. At the basin I carefully turned on the hot tap and let the water flow. The blood came off in no time. In order to ensure there was no evident I cleaned the basin with toilet paper which I flushed down the pan.

I was panting a little but I was getting my senses back. On stepping out of the bathroom, I first turned the light off then went into a bedroom at the front of the house.

The curtains over the window were open so the moonlight was illuminating the room. I went to a chest opened a drawer, extracted a t-shirt and put it on, then I stepped into a walk-in wardrobe. All his stuff was hanging up there. I took a jacket off a coat hanger. Not sure what kind it was but it was a jacket so I put it on over the t-shirt. It was a casual sports jacket not dissimilar to my own.

From here I carefully went down the stairs to collect the plastic bag containing my shirt and jacket. I paused for a few seconds. I could hear that the football game was still going on. The smell of cordite had gone. I didn't want to peer into the room to check if Drummond was still dead.

Now to leave without being seen. First, I collected my shoes and socks and carried them to the door. Jasper looked at me in the dark. He could sense that something terrible had happened in here once again. I pulled the cuff of the jacket down and used it get hold of the door handle and pull it down to open the front door a fraction. It might look odd that the front door had been left unlocked, but so what? I peered outside onto the lane beyond the row of rails. The lights of the house across the way were on. Luckily for me the security light above the front door was off. Anyone looking across to the house from that distance wouldn't see me unless they were using binoculars. I pulled the door open, grabbed Jasper's lead and quickly and carefully made my exit out of the front door. The door was closed using the cuff of the jacket. Once outside, I slipped my shoes on but placed my socks into a jacket pocket.

I walked away from the house at a quick pace but did not run. I was a bloke out on the street walking his dog after been to the local supermarket. The time was ten after nine.

It was nine-forty when I got to the shopping centre. I considered going into the store and purchasing something as a kind of alibi, but that was nonsensical. I was too tense to be angry, too worried to be elated.

There were a few rubbish skips in the car park close the supermarket. I placed the plastic bag into one of the skips. The jacket and shirt were cheap everyday clothing, nothing special. I couldn't care less about losing them.

When Carol got into the car by my side she didn't even notice that I was wearing an unfamiliar jacket and shirt or that I had no socks on. She asked me if I had heard the news that the police had found the body of a man – likely to be Michael Bovey – in Tinkers Wood wrapped in a plastic sheet. I said no then something on the lines of when did that story break?

CHAPTER 13

The police soon put two and two together and came up with four. They visited every DIY store in the county to question staff and check their till receipts. They requested they take every hour of CCTV film. The breakthrough came when one of the store managers told the police that the big lottery winner, Ray Drummond, had recently purchased a large plastic cover and several other items. Well that was it. The police had something to go on. They immediately despatched two detectives to go to Drummond's house to question him.

Of course, he wasn't in. Well he was in but he wasn't answering the door. When a detective tried the front door, they stepped in and found his body in the lounge with the gun still in his hand. A thorough investigation took place. It was quickly established that Drummond and Bovey had recently met, though the meeting in the posh restaurant out of town had been done on the quiet. Bovey had not told anyone where or who he was meeting. It was only when one of the staff recognised the picture of Bovey in a local newspaper that the connection was made.

All the neighbours in the surrounding vicinity of Drummond's home were questioned. Nobody had seen anything or anyone at the house. Drummond tended to be a bit of a loner who kept himself to himself. Few people visited him. Then the police searched the house. In the garage they found the pool cue used to kill Bovey and the blanket used to cover him. Both had his blood on them. A forensic search of the basement discovered traces of blood and hair samples which were matched to Bovey. They even found the cheque and the 'Memorandum of Intent' stuffed into the table drawer. They also found a business card with Tony Plummer's name on it. He was questioned. He confirmed that he had done some work for Drummond concerning the whereabouts of Helen Symonds, now Bovey. When asked how Drummond had got his name he said probably from the yellow pages.

The police concluded that an argument had taken place in Drummond's house which had resulted in Drummond clubbing Bovey to death with the pool cue. The circumstances of the argument would and could never be established though there was motive. Bovey intended to embezzle him out of the money. Maybe Drummond had challenged him. An argument took place with Drummond attacking him with the cue. Drummond then dragged him down to the basement where he wrapped his body in the plastic sheet he had purchased from the DIY store, then he had taken him to Tinkers Wood in his SUV. It was an open and shut case

My advice to get rid of the cheque and the, 'Memorandum of Intent' had gone unheeded. This was a blessing because the police now had connection and motive. The connection between Drummond and Helen Bovey was perhaps more difficult to explain. That was until the police looked into Drummond's past and discovered that he knew her from the time they worked together, several years ago. The police also found fragments of cotton on the barbeque grill. The fibres were examined and found to be from a disposable overall. They also found the foot coverings in the garage. Clearly Drummond had been less than careful. It was a good job that I had disposed of the items I had used and not left them with him.

When the police took everything into consideration they concluded that Drummond had killed Bovey in his house. They searched hours of CCTV taken from gardening centres in the locality and found evidence that Drummond had visited a couple of places in a short period of time during one afternoon. He had purchased the plastic sheet at one store, then the paper overalls and the parcel tape at another DIY store.

As there was no sign of a break in or a struggle or anything stolen from Drummond's home, and no evidence of anyone else been in the house, they concluded that Drummond had taken his own life by shooting himself in the chest. They calculated that Drummond had discovered the news that a body had been found, then fearing a knock at the door from the police he had taken his own life rather than face up to the music.

Drummond's funeral took place the day after Bovey's. Bovey's took place in his home city of Northampton. Drummond's was at the local crematorium. Despite the adverse publicity there was a decent turnout to see him off. Several of his and my work colleagues turned up to pay their respects. Despite the chance to quiz the mourners the press failed to turn up in numbers. The crime reporter from the local rag appeared, but that was about it.

I meet a couple of Drummond relatives. Drummond had told me that his parents had passed away before I knew him. He often spoke about staying with an uncle who lived somewhere on the south coast. He was here - Arthur Drummond - a small, bald bloke who had more than a passing resemblance to his nephew. He had an Aunt Lorna who arrived with a couple of her children, both in their thirties. He also had sister he never mentioned before.

The service was short. Not big on the religious front. His sister had chosen the music. She had selected a couple of Queen tracks: 'The Show Must Go On' and 'Your My Best Friend'. Someone who knew him from way back read a poem. The usual stuff. The entire ceremony lasted a shade over thirty minutes. The wake took place in a local pub. We munched sandwiches and silently toasted Ray Drummond.

CHAPTER 14

One week after the funeral I was disturbed by a knock at the front door. It was the postman. He handed me an official looking envelope which I had to sign for. I opened the envelope with trepidation. It contained a letter. Maybe it was a threat or letter saying that I owed someone money. The letter was on headed paper from 'Harrison, Lord and Crabbe' Solicitors. They had an office in the centre of town. I had often driven passed their place.

Anyway, I read the contents of the letter and I don't mind telling you that I was in for a bit of a surprise. A nice surprise, I hasten to add. The letter was inviting me to attend a meeting at which the last will and testament of Raymond Peter Drummond was to be read out. Oh my Lord, I said to myself. Had he left me another twenty thousand pounds? I felt thrilled then I felt a sense of anxiety because maybe this was going to be the final kick in the teeth. Rather than show the letter to Carol I stuffed it into my pocket. Later that day I contacted a young lady at the solicitors to say I would be able to make the appointment.

The appointment was for one week from today at three in the afternoon. It would mean booking an afternoon off work. In the week since the funeral and two weeks after Drummond's death I had not heard anything from the police or anyone else. The police were still concentrating on the theory that Drummond fearing that he was about to be arrested for the murder of Bovey had taken his own life with an illegal firearm. To be candid about it nobody missed him.

As for me I was keeping my head down. Carol had commented that I was becoming a house husband. Indeed, I had turned down a couple of invitations to go on a pub crawl with a couple of mates from work, and that was unusual. My excuse was that I was feeling down following Drummond's suicide. The week went quickly enough. At work we were already winding down for Christmas. Everyone including me looked forward to the Christmas break.

The week soon passed. I had booked the afternoon off work. I didn't tell Carol where I was going. When she asked me why I was wearing my best suit I said I was going for another job in the office, therefore I had decided to go prepared. After all. 'Fail to prepare - Prepare to fail' and all that.

It was two-fifty when I arrived at the office of 'Harrison, Lord and Crabbe'. Punctuality was my middle name. I entered through the front door and introduced myself to the young lady at the front reception desk, a rather pretty girl with a cute smile. She greeted me with a pleasant, 'good afternoon', and asked me to follow her. She escorted me into a small meeting room at the back of the building.

As I entered the room I clapped my eyes on three other people who were sitting in high backed chairs around a stout committee type table. There was Uncle Arthur, Aunt Lorna and his sister Rita. They like me were dressed soberly. They all eyed me as I entered the room. The walls were bright white. Sunlight was streaming in through two large windows overlooking a garden at the rear. It was the first time I had been in this building.

On the wall were framed photographs of previous solicitors who had represented the practice down the years. An open fireplace with an ornate mantel piece held a rather nice decorative clock.

In the light Uncle Arthur looked remarkably like the late Ray Drummond. He had the same fair to ginger hair though he didn't have a lot of hair remaining. The same pale, wan complexion. His Aunt Lorna was wearing a fur coat and a matching hat on her head. Rita was in black. She held a handkerchief in her hand and constantly dabbed her eyes and nose.

The young lady showed me to a seat. I was two along from Rita and directly opposite Uncle Arthur. I made eye contact with him and nodded my head. He responded in kind. The girl who had brought me into the room asked me if I wanted a drink. I said no thank you. As she turned to leave the clock on the mantle rang the hour of three. On the final chime, another door opened, and a rather portly, senior looking guy, wearing a pin striped three-piece suit, entered.

He was carrying a plain file. He was accompanied by an equally sober looking woman in tweeds who was wearing a pair of Dame Edna spectacles. It was like something out of the sixties. She was carrying a notepad and a pen. The man had a thick waistline, white hair and thick black rimmed reading glasses over his eyes.

He sat at the business end of the table. He didn't smile. This was far too serious for smiles. His colleague sat by his side. He looked up and addressed the four of us around the table.

"Good afternoon and thank you for attending this, the reading of the last will and testament of Raymond Peter Drummond." Then he opened the file and withdrew some dark yellow papers.

"Ladies and gentlemen," he began. "This is the final will and testament of the late Raymond Peter Drummond." He read from the paper.

It took him a while to get through the opening stuff, the legal terminology and the waffle. Then he got down to the serious business. The business everyone was here for. His tone of voice was measured and precise.

"I leave the following from my estate to the named persons in this will. To my uncle Ronald Arthur Drummond, I leave the sum of three million pounds." Arthur Drummond looked up. I could see his Adams apple move as the sum was read out.

"To my dear sister. Rita Karen Bird. I leave one and a half million pounds and my investment portfolio." She didn't bat an eyelid. It was like a scene from 'Kind Hearts and Coronets'. One of my favourite movies. But no one was laughing.

The chap adjusted his spectacles. His colleague was taking notes of what he was saying. He coughed. "To my dear Aunt Lorna Jane Pearson. I leave one million pounds." I looked around the table.

That just left me. The senior lawyer chap shuffled the papers. "To my good friend Stephen Lee Tomlin." That was me, though strangely enough I didn't recognise my name for a few moments. It was as if he was reading out an alien name to me. "I leave the following. My house, my two motor vehicles, my Haley Davidson motorcycle and the sum of seven hundred and fifty thousand pounds."

I could hardly comprehend what he had just said. A tear came to my eye. I don't mind telling you that I began to cry real tears. I was emotional. I had cracked. The note-taker got out of her seat. She went into the office and came back carrying a box of tissues and a glass of water. She gave me the tissues and the water. I dabbed my eyes then took a sip of water. My mate had left me three quarters of a million pounds and a house worth at least twice that. His other relatives looked at me with sympathy in their eyes. My life had just changed in the blink of an eye.

When I got home that afternoon, Carol asked me if I had got the job. I didn't reply. I asked her to sit down. What I was about to tell her was very serious. She looked at me as though I was about to tell her I wanted a divorce. I told her where I had been and why.

When I told her, what had been read out by Mister Crabbe of 'Harrison, Lord and Crabbe', she grabbed me then squealed like a child, then she screamed, and she screamed some more. After a few minutes, once she had calmed down, she asked me if it was a sick joke. No. It was no joke. We had just inherited three quarters of a million pounds, a four-bedroomed detached house in a highly desirable part of town, two high performance cars, and oh and not forgetting a top-of-the-range Harley Davidson motorcycle.

She could hardly believe it. The shock was so great she nearly fell off her seat. Our lives would only get better from this point forward. That night we cracked open a couple of tins of beer and toasted the late Raymond Drummond. I felt vindicated in a way. He had promised me his house and I had got the house. It was a shame that he had to die, but necessary as he would have shopped me at the end of the day. He would have caved in within hours and told them it was all my idea. I wouldn't have had a leg to stand on.

The following day, both Carol and I went into our places of employment and handed in our resignation notices. I requested that I be allowed to leave as soon as possible. I negotiated a two-week leave period.

CHAPTER 15

In the first week of January, I was called into the office of, 'Harrison, Lord and Crabbe'. Mister Crabbe, the gentlemen who had read the will four weeks before handed me a cheque for seven hundred and fifty thousand pounds, the deeds to the house and the keys. Along with the keys and paperwork for the BMW, the SUV, and the Harley Davidson motorcycle.

We moved into the house one week later. It felt strange for us to be in such a large house after our cramped little council house. We couldn't get used to it. It didn't feel right. I avoided the lounge as much as possible. It was eerie. It wasn't long before we moved out into a rented house. We put the house up for sale the following month. It went on the market for fifty pounds shy of one and a half million. It sold two months later for one point seven five million pounds.

We had our eye on a cottage on the other side of town not too far from Tinkers Wood. We sold the BMW and the SUV. We bought a much smaller car.

Then exactly one year to the day after the death of Ray Drummond, Carol gave birth to twins. A boy and a girl. We named our son Luke Andrew Tomlin, and named our daughter Laura Charlotte Tomlin. Our family was complete.

I never did bump into Helen Bovey. I heard that she had to sell up and move out of her home as her husband had stolen the best part of six hundred thousand pounds from his clients. She had to pay it back.

I don't know why I was concerned about her. Maybe it was because it all began with her. Maybe it was because I did feel a little bit of guilt. That would pass. And rest assured it did.

The End

The Collector

CHAPTER 1

Maybe it was because Kilbane didn't believe in karma that he agreed to do it. Or, maybe it was because he didn't have a lot of choice in the matter. When all was said and done it was the latter.

Like a lot of people who have an addiction to a vice of one sort or other, David Kilbane couldn't let it go. He wasn't addicted to drugs or booze or anything that would do his body harm. He wasn't addicted to internet porn or anything that would eat into his soul and make him a vile human being. His vice was gambling. His preferred poison was betting on the outcomes of football games. English premier league matches. He knew the teams, their goals for and against, the players, the coaches, and the managers. He knew how the league table was stacked. He used all this knowledge to try and predict the outcomes of games. He was good at it. Or so he thought. He had made money. The problem was that sometimes he was down and when he was down the chasm could be deep. If that wasn't bad enough he had begun to borrow money to gamble. If he won, he paid it back within a day or two, but his luck had been out for a couple of weeks. He owed money, not a huge amount in the grand scheme of things, but he still owed money to a lender who wanted it back. This lender was no high street bank willing to provide him with a quick loan at a generous rate of interest. This was a money lender who didn't play the game by the rules laid down by the Financial Services Authority. At the last count Kilbane owed two and a half thousand pounds.

He had avoided the money lenders hangouts in and around the East-End of London. He did anticipate a text message sometime soon asking him to meet with the lender to settle the debt. The trouble was he didn't have the money. His recent bad luck meant he didn't have much more than four hundred pounds to his name. After all who would predict that West Ham would go to White Hart Lane and do Tottenham three-zip on their own patch?

If he didn't pay the money back in the next day the debt would increase ten per cent daily. By the end of the week the debt would be as much as four thousand, nine hundred pounds. His lender wasn't the kind of person who would listen to a sob story. If Kilbane didn't face the music and pay up he was the kind of lender who would send his heavies around to have a word. Then if he still didn't pay his heavies would invite him to an early morning meeting with their boss who would be happy to put Kilbane's hand into a vice and cut off one of his little fingers. They were not nice people. The thought of losing a finger made him cringe.

He had several options; one was to find the money as soon as possible. The second was to contact the lender and explain the situation to him. Another option was to go on the run. Where could he run with four hundred pounds in his pocket? Another option was to try and cover the debt by borrowing from someone else. That would be like robbing Peter to pay Paul. He could always stick up a post-office, but he didn't have the bottle to do that. He would probably cock-it-up big style and become a right laughing stock.

He thought better of that idea. He did consider his options and came to the rather brave decision to call the lender to inform him of his cash flow problems and to face the music. The lender might be sympathetic – he may have found God – or enlightenment, though Kilbane doubted that. Maybe he would give him more time to find the cash. To do nothing and to let the debt build until it doubled in size wasn't a sensible option. On this occasion, common-sense prevailed. Kilbane made the call to Bron.

Bron was surprisingly receptive to Kilbane's admission that he didn't have the money. He told Kilbane he wanted to talk to him to see if they could work it out in an adult-to-adult manner and accommodate his late payment. Rather than issue threats he suggested that they meet, and to show him he had no intention of doing him harm, he agreed to meet him in a neutral venue. A pub in Upton Park. A place they both knew. Kilbane was put at rest. Though he did wonder why Bron came across as so understanding. It wasn't his style. He tended to issue threats of dire consequences if the money wasn't forthcoming. Not an invitation to drinks in a well-known East-End boozer.

CHAPTER 2

Kilbane met Bron in the, 'Duke of Edinburgh', public house on Green Street in Upton Park. This neighbourhood was Kilbane's old stamping ground. He had been brought up on these streets, so he knew the area. He had followed the local football team - West Ham United - from an early age and still did today though he didn't manage to see many games; such was the cost of watching football these days. This area of London's East-End was his neighbourhood. He had, for several years, attended a local Judo club. He had achieved a black belt first Dan grade. He was still handy and knew the moves and how to defend himself. He was a little tournament rusty, but he was still able to throw most people.

Even though it was only three-thirty in the afternoon the lights in the convenience stores, the clothes' stores and the fast-food parlours were coming on. Kilbane detested this time of the year. The run-up to Christmas. All the false joy and wishing everyone a merry Christmas made him want to puke. He didn't mind the actual Christmas week. It was the fact that it began weeks before that irked him.

The, 'Duke of Edinburgh', was in a spot just a decent goal-kick away from the old Boleyn Ground, the ancestral home of the Hammers, before they relocated the couple of miles to the Olympic Stadium. The walls of the pub were decorated with glass framed pictures of Hammers' heroes from the past along with the cross Irons symbol on the club's crest.

The wide screen TV over the bar was showing Greyhound racing from some God-forsaken place up north. A juke box was playing. The volume was so low it was impossible to recognise the track.

The pub wasn't well frequented at this time in the afternoon. A reflection of the fact that times were hard. Few people had money to spend on pub price booze. As Kilbane entered the guy behind the bar observed him and nodded his head, though Kilbane didn't know him from Adam.

Kilbane glanced around. The people he had come to see where sitting huddled around a table in an alcove, below a large glass framed photograph of England's 1966 World Cup hero - the one and only - the late, great Bobby Moore.

There was Bron. His side-kick come bodyguard Fat Tony was by his side. They were good East-End boys turned bad. Kind of low-life gangsters. They had pints in their hands. They observed Kilbane enter the pub and go to the bar.

Aaron Bron was your archetypical low-life, scum-bag loan-shark. He was a street fighter who didn't use Marquis of Queensbury rules. He probably thought the Marquis owned Harrods. He was all black leather and bravado. A hard man who used even harder men for backup. He financed people who had no truck at the bank. If you welched on a deal or failed to pay him back within the agreed time limit, then you could expect a nasty wake-up call at three o'clock in the morning. Some say he had made his money through a people smuggling racket, then had got into the backstreet loan game when people smuggling was taken over by foreign mafia types and a whole set of bad mother-fuckers. His interest rates weren't bad. It was just that he had little sense of humour if you didn't pay him back on time.

He loved his black leather jacket and his machismo look. He modelled himself on a young Al Pacino. His favourite movie was, 'Scarface'.

He was unshaven with a couple of days growth around his chin. Dark hair, now receding from the forehead. The light on the wall above was reflecting in his widening centre parting. Mean looking eyes and a pot marked face. His eyes had a piercing quality. Some may say he was a good-looking guy. Six feet four, slim and fit. He had the physique of someone who played rugby for he was nimble on his feet and quick off the mark.

He eyed Kilbane as did Fat Tony. Fat Tony was called Fat Tony because of his uncanny resemblance to the character of the same name in the Simpsons' cartoons.

Kilbane bought a pint from the bar and came towards the table with the pot in his hand. He sat down in a spare seat and put his beer on the table top.

Bron didn't waste any time with introductions.

"Where's my money?" he asked.

Kilbane took a sip of his beer. Fat Tony watched him from near. Far too close for comfort. Fat Tony could easily reach out, grab him around the neck and put him in a headlock. In the short-sleeved t-shirt Tony's tattooed arms were clearly visible. His biceps were like thick joints of prime beef. If Tony put you in a choke-hold he could force the air out of your lungs in less than a minute. By one minute and ten seconds your life would be flashing by your eyes. Kilbane feared that Bron would give him the nod. Tony would grab him and there was little he could do except to try and throw him.

"I'm having a little cash flow problem right now," said Kilbane, in reply to Bron's question. His words were accompanied by a smile. "I'll have it shortly, though."

Bron looked at him. His expression remained sullen. Nothing. He continued to give him that look. He wasn't amused. Kilbane feared the nod, then the sensation of Fat Tony's huge arms grasping him around his neck. The nod didn't come.

"Oh dear. I'm so sorry to hear that. But I'm pleased you've told me," said Bron. He took his pint pot and lifted it to his lips. He took in a small quantity of the amber liquid. "Yeah, that saddens me. You know my rates, don't you?"

"I do," Kilbane replied. "Ten per cent a day, rising to twenty after ten days."

"You owe me two and a half K. When do you think you'll have it for me?" He looked to Fat Tony and nodded his head. Kilbane was ready to fight off the headlock. It never came. Tony eyed Kilbane. He brushed his hair away from his face. His breath smelled of something repugnant. Like something you'd find at the bottom of a dustbin.

"I don't know Aaron. Maybe another week," said Kilbane.

"Maybe, isn't good enough. You know what happens to late payers don't you? Tony gets annoyed." Tony grunted, right on cue.

"I'll have the money with you shortly," said Kilbane.

Bron sat back and seemed to relax. His eyes went around the bar.

"You know I'm pleased you've come to see him. You've done the right thing." He looked at Kilbane and tilted his head to one side. "Seriously you've done the right thing. What if you do something for me and we'll forget all about the debt."

Kilbane was surprised, then again maybe he wasn't because Bron could be unpredictable. But did he just say something about forgetting the debt?

"What is it?" he asked.

Bron smiled a cheesy grin. He could see that he had thrown Kilbane a lifeline and he seemed keen to grasp it. Bron edged forward. He took his pint glass and held it just inches from his lips. His voice was hushed. His eyes went to the other set of drinkers at the far end of the room.

"There's a man in Amsterdam I want you to go and see. He's got a package for me. What say you go to Amsterdam and collect it for me?" he said.

"A collector!" Kilbane asked.

Alarm bells began to ring in his head. The word, 'collect' seemed to stick out like a big sore thumb. It reverberated through his head and came out with a huge warning sign attached to it.

"What kind of package. What's in it?" he asked.

Bron sat back and opened out his wide chest.

"Why the questions? Don't you want to get rid of your debt by doing me this one little favour?" he asked.

Kilbane didn't answer the question immediately. He sucked on it like he was sucking on a grapefruit. He didn't like the taste. It was sour and bitter at the same time.

"I'd have to know what's in the package," he said.

"Something very close to my heart. Something I desire," said Bron.

Fat Tony smirked, then he looked at Kilbane and his body language stiffened. Just then someone entered the bar and came to the table. It was Ronnie Taylor, another one of Bron's acolytes. He parked himself at the table. Bron looked at him.

"Ronnie. I've just asked our friend here if he'd like to go to Amsterdam to collect the package. He doesn't seem to like the idea."

"The fuck he doesn't" said Taylor. "Go to Amsterdam and pick up the package you friggin wuss."

Bron's eyes clamped onto Kilbane. "I don't think he's got a choice. It's either that or Tony will cut off his fingers with a blunt hacksaw."

Never a truer word had been said. The package. What was it? Kilbane asked himself. He wasn't going to ask Bron again. Was it drugs? Laundered money? He didn't have a clue. Perhaps the only thing he could do was to go. Collect the package then he might be able to discover what was inside. He didn't have a lot of wriggle room.

"Okay, I'll collect the package for you, but as a matter of interest why can't you collect it?" he asked.

Bron spread his arms wide. "Why the fuck would I want to leave all this?" he said in a sarcastic manner. Fat Tony stifled a chuckle. "I've got a record as long as a porn-stars dick. I'd love to go, but why have all the hassle when you can go instead. Anyway, why you welching? Do you want Tony to give you a free manicure or summat?"

Kilbane sighed. "Okay. I'll go to Amsterdam to collect the package. And my debt has gone?" he said with a question in the tone.

"Eh. Don't you trust us?" bellowed Fat Tony. His voice was as gruff as a bad case of laryngitis.

"Who do I need to see?" Kilbane asked.

"All in good time," said Bron. He downed the remaining lager in one visit to his mouth. "Barman another round of drinks," he requested aloud.

Kilbane took time to think. If he went and brought the package back the debt would be gone and he would keep his fingers. It was a no-brainer. He had to go to Amsterdam to collect the package and bring it back to London.

"Who do I need to see?" he asked.

"A guy called Peter DeGroot," Bron replied.

"DeGroot?"

"Yes DeGroot. He's a *cloggie* for fuck sake."

"Where do I find this DeGroot?" Kilbane asked.

Bron dipped a hand into an inside jacket pocket. He extracted a small piece of plain white paper which he handed to Kilbane. Kilbane opened the sheet and read what was written on it.

PETER DEGROOT

210b Damrak

AMSTERDAM

Tel 023 346 7456

"He's expecting you in two days. Tell him the London team sent you for the package and he'll give it to you. Bring it back here. We'll be waiting for you. If you deliver the package safely your debt will be paid."

Kilbane slipped the paper in his jacket pocket. "What happens if DeGroot doesn't give me the package?" he asked.

"For fuck sake," said Taylor. "Your mutton or summat? He'll be expecting you. Take the package from him and come straight back to London. No friggin sightseeing. Come straight back here."

Bron blinked. "DeGroot will contact us here to tell us you've been to collect it. Now piss-off and pack. You've got a train and a ferry to catch. There's a boat train leaving from Liverpool Street tomorrow afternoon at two o'clock. Be on it."

"And we don't want a friggin postcard," said Taylor.

They all laughed out loud. Fat Tony was so boisterous that his laugh filled the room. The other drinkers looked in his direction until Taylor gave them a blank stare. They soon looked the other way and got on with their business.

The barman came across the room with a tray in his hands and deposited another round of drinks on the table. Kilbane didn't hang about. He wasn't invited to stay for another pint.

CHAPTER 3

Two days later

A cold, chilly breeze was blowing along Damrak. The canal tour-boats in Dam dock were bobbing in the choppy, colourless water. The ropes securing them to a pontoon were stretching out into the dock and straining to the very end of their sinews. On such a dreary, chilly morning at ten-thirty with hardly any natural light the centre of Amsterdam looked like the cold, drab, colourless, slate-grey backdrop to some bleak art-house movie. The Christmas lights and garish neon from the store fronts along the long thoroughfare were hardly strong enough to penetrate the gloom. A trolley bus glided along the street.

Kilbane hadn't been in Amsterdam for over ten years. The last time was on a stag-do with a load of mates from the East-End. It was summer then. Now in the cold, dark light of a dreary December day it looked less than inviting. Like a wet weekend in Clacton. He couldn't recall a great deal about that trip, other than the red-light district and a couple of bars he had been in and the live sex show they had attended when the condemned man – the groom – received a favour from one of the strippers. It was a right laugh. Now ten years older, but none the wiser, at thirty-eight-years-of-age he was back on a different mission. He often wondered where his mates had disappeared to. He hadn't seen the groom for about five years. Unlike the groom, Kilbane had stayed clear of the marrying game.

He wondered what the package would be like. Its size, shape, and weight. Whether it would come gift wrapped or if it would be handed to him in a bag of some description. He didn't know what it was.

He ascended the short flight of stairs to the door of a sex-shop on the first floor of the building at 210b Damrak. It was a tiny store, not much bigger than a small room. It was stacked high with a whole array of pornographic magazines. In floor to waist high glass cabinets were a display of sex toys, from dildos and vibrators to all kinds of things Kilbane had never seen before. There were even some whips for the S&M brigade along with gimp masks and more play wear. It was strange to say the least.

He stepped the four paces to the counter where a man was standing browsing through the pages of a glossy magazine. Techno pop music was playing on a radio perched on the counter. The man raised his head as Kilbane approached him.

"Ja." He closed the pages of the magazine.

"Are you Peter DeGroot?" Kilbane asked.

The man said nothing, but his body language told Kilbane he had found DeGroot. He was a short guy. Aged around fifty-years-of-age. A thick midriff tapered up a narrow torso to a thin neck and small head. He wore black rimmed spectacles over bloodshot eyes. He was bald but insisted on trying to disguise it by combing a few strands of hair across his skull. He was wearing a spangled waistcoat over a purple shirt. Brown cord slacks were held up by a thin belt. He eyed the visitor.

"Can I help you?" he asked. His English was good, though delivered in a thick Dutch accent.

"I'm Kilbane," said Kilbane. DeGroot looked at him closely as if he did not understand. "The package for Aaron Bron. The London team. I've come for the package. I'm the collector," he said slowly and deliberately.

"Oh the package. Just a moment," said DeGroot. He didn't utter another word. He turned back, stepped through an open doorway and went out of view. Meanwhile a customer entered the shop and began to browse amongst the dirty magazines. Kilbane waited at the counter. He could hear a conversation in the rear of the establishment. In Dutch he assumed, though he couldn't be certain. It could have been English. He couldn't hear well enough above the sound of music coming out of the radio.

It was another thirty seconds before DeGroot emerged. He was followed by a girl of around fifteen-or-sixteen-years-of-age who was wearing a kind of post punk outfit. A loud, image stencilled dark t-shirt and tight thigh length denim shorts over dark tights. Her make-up was thick with plenty of mascara around her eyes. Her lips were the shade of coal. She wore a ring through her left nostril. When she opened her mouth a metal brace along the top row of her teeth was visible, along with the stud in her tongue. Her hair was arranged into two long plats that fell over her shoulders. She was small boned. Not much taller than five feet tall. Very thin. Not at all attractive. She was chewing gum in a loud and aggressive manner. If chewing gum was an Olympic sport she would be in the Dutch team. Her jaws moved with the power of pistons.

The man who had been flicking through the magazines left as soon as the girl appeared. Interestingly, DeGroot wasn't carrying anything. Kilbane looked at him and wondered where the package was. The girl looked at Kilbane. Kilbane looked at DeGroot. DeGroot looked at the girl. A stony silence descended.

It was Kilbane who broke the silence. "The package. Where is it?" he enquired and held his hand out as though he was expecting to be handed something.

"This is the package," said De Groot.

Kilbane was confused. "W…What?" he stammered.

DeGroot glanced at the girl. "She's the package," he said.

"Oh, for fucks sake," said Kilbane.

The girl 'tutted' out loud. "If you don't mind my name is Kiri. For your information I'm not a package."

She spoke English without an accent. She was from the north of England. Manchester or Liverpool, or the area in-between.

"What the fuck?" said Kilbane.

DeGroot looked mortified. "Didn't *he* tell you? You are to take her to England." The '*he*' he referred to could have been Aaron Bron.

"Did he bollocks," snapped Kilbane.

DeGroot looked nonplussed by this exchange. "This is the girl you have to take to London. Here are your tickets." He reached under the counter and handed Kilbane an A5 size white envelope.

Kilbane took it out of his hand. The girl continued to chew the gum and observe his body language. Her eyes were narrow. She looked at Kilbane with little expression on her face. The ring in her nose glinted.

There was no writing on the envelope. Kilbane ripped it open along the seal and extracted the contents. The envelope contained a hand-written note, two sets of train tickets, tickets for the Hook of Holland to Harwich ferry and an EU UK passport. He looked at the last page of the passport. It was her passport. It said her name was Kiri Porter. She was a British citizen. Her place of birth said, Manchester. The photograph was of her in her pre-post-modern punk appearance. It gave a date of birth that suggested she was seventeen-years- of-age. He said *suggested* because if anything she looked younger than seventeen. The envelope also contained four hundred Euros in banknotes.

Oh my god, Kilbane said to himself. She was the package he had to take back to London. What did she have that was so important to Bron? So valuable that he was prepared to write off the debt on her safe delivery? The truth was that he didn't have a clue.

He looked at DeGroot, then at Kiri. She was absently, almost unconsciously turning over the plats of her hair as if it was some kind of a habit, whilst she looked at Kilbane and continued to chew the gum and smack her lips. Kilbane blasphemed to himself. Had his life come to this? Were he was playing nursemaid to some anaemic, adolescent punk kid?

She was holding a sports bag type of holdall. It looked full to bursting. It was just an everyday sports bag with a trademark logo and symbol splashed across it. It must have weighed a few kilos because she had to put it down on the counter top. It also looked brand new. It hit the glass counter with a heavy thud.

He looked at the travel tickets. They were train and ferry tickets. The first leg was the four o'clock train from Amsterdam to the Hook of Holland, then an eight o'clock ferry to Harwich, then once on the other side of the English Channel a train journey of two hours to Liverpool Street. He would be home at around four tomorrow morning.

He needed this like he needed a new hole in his arse. What in God's name was he going to do with this new age punk in tow? The time was ten to eleven, therefore he had the best part of five hours to kill. What was he going to do for five hours? Visit the art museums? Take a look around the Anne Frank house? No, he didn't think so.

Kilbane stepped down the steps onto Damrak and glanced around, wondering which way to go. Kiri was a few yards behind him with her possessions in the bag. He stopped and waited until she had caught up. He looked at this surly kid.

"What do you want to do?" he snapped.

"Dun 'know," she replied. "Whatever."

He tutted. "Well think of something."

"How about a drink?" she asked. "A beer." She swung the bag around her shoulders and gave him attitude. As if she was showing him her strength. As if she was a ladette.

"No, I don't think so," he said.

He looked at the tour boats lined up in the dock. A group of tourists, who were well wrapped up against the cold, were standing in a queue at the ticket booth. The first tour was about to commence in twenty minutes at a quarter past eleven.

"Come on. This should kill some time. We'll go on a tour of the canals. When in Amsterdam and all that," he said.

It would be a novelty and he could keep his eyes or her. He didn't want her wandering off. He had come all this way to take her back to London. He intended on doing just that. She didn't seem keen; nevertheless, she followed him to the ticket booth where they queued for tickets.

CHAPTER 4

For the next two and a half hours they went on a sightseeing trip of the famous Amsterdam canals in a glass topped boat. It was the quintessential Amsterdam experience. Meandering through the canals, under the bridges, looking at the buildings and places of interest. An on-board tour guide provided an interesting; if over long commentary, on all the sights and places of interest along the route. Throughout the tour they didn't say a lot to each other. She was just a kid. She didn't particularly enjoy it and neither did he. They were like a father and bored teenage daughter combination.

He tried to start a conversation, but she didn't take the bait or seem interested. What she did tell him was that she was from the Mosside area of Manchester. She had come to Amsterdam one year before to live in a hippy commune across the river in north Amsterdam. She didn't volunteer much more, other than she had been asked by a man she worked for to go to London with a stranger. Once she was in London another man would give her two thousand pounds, then she could return to Amsterdam if she wished. When Kilbane asked her what she did here she went all coy on him, but soon admitted that she worked as a 'go-go' dancer in a club. Kilbane was astounded. He didn't see that one coming. She seemed quite vulnerable but also street-wise at the same time, like a hard-ass kid. Kids grew up fast on the streets of Mosside.

He tried to press her about her parents or guardians, but she put up a shutter to him and played him with a straight bat. Anyway, it was nothing to do with him. He changed the subject. He tried to get more information from her about the man who had asked her to make the trip to London with him, but she was no committal. Clearly, she had been told to avoid giving answers to those types of questions. All she knew was that she had to go to London with the man she would meet in the shop at 210b Damrak, and that he would take her to London to meet a stranger who would give her two thousand pounds.

Kilbane noticed how she kept a tight hold of her bag. Maybe it contained all her possessions. Or maybe it contained something else. While he did not feel much of a connection to her, he had only met her a few hours ago, he no longer felt the animosity towards her as he had felt at the outset.

By the end of the boat tour Kilbane was a little bit wiser but still none the wiser in a lot of respects. As they climbed out of the boat and walked along the wooden pontoon the time was getting on for two o'clock. They would leave for the railway station in one hour from now. From the dock at Damrak they sauntered towards Dam Square. Kiri said she wanted a coffee. With four hundred Euros in his pocket Kilbane said they had enough for a coffee and something to eat.

It was Kiri who suggested they visit a coffee bar a minute from Dam Square. She told Kilbane it was a place she knew well and had frequented on numerous occasions. He said okay. They ventured along the narrow side street that ran from Dam Square to the inner canal and the area of Wallen. She led the way along a canal side, passed a few licenced premises and came to a café with chairs and tables outside and a canopy over the front to shield the patrons from the elements. The tables and chairs set out at the front were un-occupied. The cold nip in the air meant that only those who were warmly dressed would sit outside for any length of time. The canal was just ten yards across the narrow path and the cobbled street which was only wide enough for one vehicle to negotiate. A houseboat on the canal was tied by a rope secured to a metal ring embedded in the concrete.

She entered the café first. Kilbane was a few paces behind her. It was a typical Amsterdam coffee shop. A set of four tables and chairs were in the interior, so it wasn't a large space. A glass counter contained all sorts of weird and wonderful cakes. An aroma of freshly ground coffee beans filled the interior. A couple of customers were sitting at a table. One reading a paperback novel, the other nibbling on a savoury bite. A Paloma Faith track was playing out of a speaker high up on the wall.

Kilbane went to the counter. Kiri placed her bag down on a table then said she was going outside to roll a cigarette. He didn't reply. He looked at the cake options behind the glass counter, then at the board displaying the various types of coffee and the price in Euros. He concentrated on ordering a drink and something to eat.

He assumed that she was sitting at one of the tables by the side of the canal. It wasn't until he glanced around that he saw that she wasn't at a table nor was she standing in the doorway. A car had stopped on the road directly outside of the shop front. He didn't think a lot about it and looked back at the coffee options once again. There was too much choice. Nothing in this world was simple anymore.

An assistant behind the counter asked him, in English, what he would like to order. He said he'd have two medium straight coffees and two pieces of that carrot cake. He was about to turn around to ask Kiri if that was okay when the sound of a car door slamming, then the screech of tyres on the cobbled surface grabbed his attention. He didn't know what was going on. He stepped out of the doorway to see the back of a car accelerating up the cobbled incline to the junction at the top. Through the back window he could see Kiri in the back seat. A figure was beside her. She had turned her head to look back. She had her arms up, hands raised, as if she was clawing at the glass or fighting with the person at her side. She had gone in the blink of an eye. He watched the car. It was a large, bronze-brown coloured, old type of Mercedes with lots of chrome bumper. At the top of the incline it turned right onto the street, crossed over the hump of a bridge to the other side of the canal and went out of view. She was gone before he could do anything. *What the fuck had just happened?* he asked himself.

Suddenly a stranger appeared at his side. He was a man in his forties. Medium build and stature. He had a serious, concerned look on his face, as if he had just witnessed something disturbing. He had thick dark hair. He was wearing a heavy padded, puffer type jacket. Spectacles over his eyes. He came to Kilbane.

"I saw it," he said tersely.

"Saw what?" Kilbane asked.

"That girl. She was standing by the side of the canal rolling a cigarette. That car stopped, two men got out, grabbed her and bundled her onto the back seat." He man pointed in the direction the car had taken.

"Fucking hell," exclaimed Kilbane.

"I got the registration," said the man. "It was Dutch registration. XJ-BR-05." The man spoke English without an accent.

Kilbane was in a quandary. It took him a few seconds to register what the man had said and to collect his thoughts.

"Oh right." He asked the man to repeat the registration.

"XJ-BR-05," he repeated. The stranger took out a scrap of paper from his jacket pocket and a pen. He wrote the number onto the paper and handed it to Kilbane.

"Thanks," said Kilbane.

"No problem. Who is she?" the stranger asked.

"Who?" Kilbane asked.

The stranger looked at him with a questioning face. "The girl."

"Oh. A friend," he replied as if it was an afterthought.

"All right," said the man. He looked at Kilbane and they looked at each other for a few seconds. "Are you going to the police?" the man asked.

"Yeah. Sure…right," said Kilbane, in a stuttering fashion. As if he didn't know what to do. It had been so sudden.

The man seemed to be ill-at-ease with his reaction. Perhaps he concluded that this was nothing to do with him. He said something on the line of, be seeing you, then he walked away from Kilbane and never turned around to look back at him.

Kilbane was stunned. Unable to grasp the reality that the girl had been snatched off the street in plain sight. What in God's name was all this about? He didn't have a clue. He had to think on his feet. He had to get the girl back. How?

The man who had given him the registration was walking away from him at a swift pace. He went up the incline, around the corner and quickly disappeared into a crowd of tourists standing on the corner. Kilbane could only remain glued to the spot. He looked at the paper in his hand. He could hardly go to the police. They would ask him too many questions. An idea came to him. He would go to see Peter DeGroot. After all, he was the only person he knew. First, he returned into the café and asked the girl behind the counter if she would look after his and Kiri's bag for ten minutes. She reluctantly said okay. He handed her a twenty Euro note for her trouble.

He made it back to Dam Square in less than five minutes, passing the pavement daffodil sellers and the covered market stalls along the stretch of Damrak.

On entering the tiny store at 210b Damrak, De Groot raised his head to look at Kilbane as if he was surprised to see him back so soon. He could see by the look on Kilbane's face that something was amiss.

"What you want?" he asked in a less than welcoming tone of voice.

There were no customers in the shop. Kilbane felt an anger come over him. As soon as he got within range he reached out and grabbed DeGroot by the lapels of his spangly waistcoat and pulled him towards him. The force nearly propelled him over the counter. DeGroot could see that he was serious. His face squirmed into a fearful aghast expression.

"Ahhhh," he spit out.

Kilbane lessoned the ferocity of his grasp, but still had hold of him.

"What the fuck is going on? Who's got her?"

"What you talk about?" DeGroot asked.

"Someone's got the girl. Snatched her off the street." He slammed the heel of his clenched fist onto the counter top, nearly smashing the glass cover.

DeGroot looked fearful and scared. "I don't know," he protested.

"What has she got?" Kilbane asked.

"I don't know," he repeated in a perplexed tone of voice.

"I think you do," said Kilbane.

"All I know is that she was brought here."

"By who?"

"By a man called Eric Petters."

"Who is Eric Petters?" Kilbane asked.

"He owns places in De Wallen."

"What places?"

"Sex show theatres."

"Get your coat."

"Why?" he asked.

"We're going to pay him a visit," said Kilbane.

"What?"

"You heard. Get your fucking coat. And you'd better start doing some explaining." Kilbane literally frogmarched DeGroot out of the store, down the stairs and onto the pavement.

The pair of them walked side-by-side for five hundred yards, through a maze of narrow streets, then onto the first canal side and along the cobbled street passing numerous coffee bars. There was a whiff of burning marijuana joints in the air.

CHAPTER 5

The red-light district of De Wallen was usually deserted in the daytime. The punters, hedonists, and the curious tended to descend on the area when the sun went down. Partly because they had no wish to be seen lurking around this area during the day but also to enjoy the array of neon and noise from the various establishments that come alive as soon as the night drew in. Many came here to observe the sight of the prostitutes standing or sitting in the windows under red lights, hence the red-light area.

DeGroot led Kilbane along a canal side pavement. A tour boat was coming by. At this hour it was less than a quarter full. The sky was still slate grey and bleak. A breeze had enough strength to send discarded sheets of newspaper fluttering down the street.

After two hundred yards they came to the entrance of a sex show theatre. Over the entrance it said, 'The Eros Review', then underneath that, 'Live Sex Show', in bold lettering.

The venue looked closed at this hour. There was a display in glass panels, on both sides of the entrance, welcoming the customers and extolling some of the virtues of the performers with words in English, French and German.

DeGroot pressed a button in an intercom unit. Someone responded almost immediately. DeGroot spoke Dutch. He could have been saying anything. Perhaps he was tipping someone off that a mad Englishman was looking for Eric Petters. Kilbane had no idea.

DeGroot stopped talking. The person at the other end said a few words, then there was silence. DeGroot stepped back a pace.

"What are you saying?" Kilbane asked.

"Petters is here. We shall talk to him," said DeGroot.

Within a matter of a few moments there was a sound of a metal bar being pushed down from the inside. One of the doors opened and a rather large blonde, German looking man appeared. He had a massive head on wide shoulders. His chin and face looked as if they had been chipped straight from granite. He held the door open. DeGroot had no hesitation about entering. He stepped inside the door. Kilbane followed him. They were in the inner sanctum of the club, in the area where the customers paid for their entertainment at a pay-booth window. It said thirty Euros each.

Ahead was an open archway leading into the performance area. To the right a set of narrow stairs winded up to the first floor. On the wall by the side of the stairs it said, 'Live Sex this way', with an arrow in the shape of an erect penis pointing upwards. It was incredibly tactless but got the message across.

The guy who opened the front door, closed the door behind him, then came forward. He must have been six feet five tall and nearly three feet wide. Kilbane wouldn't have been able to fight him off though he could have given him a run for his money. He was still a black belt, but this guy was huge. He had thick arms, a barrel chest and a face that was full of blunt features. Apparently, his name was Hans.

Hans led the way through the open archway and they came out into an open area with a bar on the right-hand side, from where the punters could buy overpriced alcohol before, during and after the show. There was an open area with half a dozen or more round tables and stools. A set of short stairs led down into a seated area with cinema style seats set out in a rigid theatre style on three sides of a stage. The stage must have been about twenty feet wide by twelve feet deep. Above it was a single rig holding the spotlights. There were at a guess sixty seats in three rows on a terraced incline to the walls.

Hans muttered something in Dutch to DeGroot, then he stepped away and went behind the bar.

DeGroot turned to look at Kilbane. "He said wait here. Petters will be down shortly," he said. Kilbane looked around the joint. So far so good. It didn't appear as if DeGroot or Hans had any nasty surprises in store for him.

From what he recalled from the time he had last been in a place like this the punters would enjoy five or six girls playing with themselves with vibrators or dildos. One of the punters might even be invited onto the stage to take part. It was all crude, tasteless and close to the bone stuff. The performance usually finished with a novelty act where some grossly obese girl would let it all out. From here the punters would be directed upstairs for the live sex where the guys and girls would screw in all kinds of ways. Thirty Euros for sixty minutes entertainment was as good as it got.

It was another minute before Hans returned. He was accompanied by a much smaller man who was dressed in snazzy dark clothing. He must have been ten stones wringing wet. He had a thin pencil beam moustache above his top lip. Dark hair was swept back over his skull. The kind of person; who, if you saw him on the street, you might take a second glance. This must have been Eric Petters.

He didn't look pleased that DeGroot had come calling. He said something to DeGroot with a sharp edge in his voice and gestured with his hands in a semi aggressive, threatening manner.

De Groot responded in much the same way. They babbled back and forth in Dutch, while Kilbane and the blonde guy looked on. The conversation appeared to be becoming increasingly heated. Clearly the man who was Eric Petters wasn't pleased about something. More than likely it was the fact that he had brought Kilbane here. He glanced at him fleetingly. His face did indicate that it wasn't one of welcome.

"What's he saying?" asked Kilbane.

"Just a moment," said Petters.

DeGroot looked to Kilbane. His comb-over looked as if it was about to slip off the top of his skull. "He doesn't know where the girl is or who has taken her," he said.

Petters looked to Kilbane. "I have no idea where she is," he said in English. His accent suggested he was more German than Dutch. His words didn't have a Dutch edge to them.

"How do you know her?" asked Kilbane.

Petters looked at him but choose not to reply. Kilbane was convinced that there was a lot more to this than met the eye. It wasn't simply a case of taking a girl back to London. There was a good reason why she had to be in London. A girl wasn't snatched off the street for no good reason. What was it? Neither Petters nor DeGroot were about to volunteer the information.

Kilbane thought it was about time to inform them that he had the registration number of the car and a description. He dipped his hand into his jacket pocket and pulled out the sheet of paper with XJ-BR-05 scribbled on it.

"This is the registration of the car she was forced into. It's a brown, old-style Mercedes 280E sedan".

He handed the paper to Petters and observed his body language. If he did recognise the registration number, he didn't reveal it. Petters said something to Hans. It wasn't in English or Dutch. It sounded German. Hans took the paper and immediately turned and went away.

"Where's he going?" asked Kilbane.

"He's going to contact someone in the local police and ask him to put a trace on the registration."

"Okay, Fine," Kilbane relented.

Petters looked at him. "Tell me," he said then unconsciously ran his hand over the back of his head before glancing around the floor. "Where is her bag?" he asked in a hushed tone.

"Whose bag?" Kilbane asked.

"The girl?" Petters replied. He looked at Kilbane in wider eyed anticipation.

Why was he so interested in her bag? Kilbane asked himself. "In the café where she left it."

He seemed relieved by the reply. "That is good."

Kilbane didn't ask him why that was good or why he wanted to know about the bag. Still, the answer seemed to make him a dam sight more relieved than he had been two minutes ago.

Petters asked Kilbane where he was staying. Kilbane told him he wasn't staying anywhere. The plan was for him to be on the four o'clock train to the Hook of Holland. Petters suggested that he forgot about that and that he go and get Kiri's bag and bring it here. Kilbane said he would think about it. Petters appeared to be disappointed by his response. He suggested to Kilbane that he find a place to stay for the night and even offered him some advice on where to go. He clearly didn't want Kilbane to leave Amsterdam without telling him where the bag was. Petters said he should stay and help to find Kiri. Kilbane wondered if Petters or DeGroot already knew where she was. He said okay. He would hang about for a while and see if he could find her.

Petters asked for Kilbane's mobile telephone number, which Kilbane gave him. Petters said he would keep in touch and contact him should anything emerge from the call to the local police station. DeGroot and Kilbane left the 'Eros Review' bar several minutes later.

CHAPTER 6

Kilbane walked back to the café where he had left the bags. In the five minutes it took him he thought long and hard about what to do next. The time was nearly three o'clock. The train would be leaving for the Hook of Holland in one hour from now. He couldn't leave without Kiri. He had to take her back. That was the deal. He decided at that point to hang around and try to find her.

He still had three hundred Euros on him. He could easily find a cheap hotel for the night. He would give it a day, then if he had not found the girl, he would decide what to do. He knew he had to get away from this area. He walked into Dam Square then onto Rokin, which continued onto Singel. On Singel he turned down by the flower market adjacent to a canal. It was picture postcard Amsterdam. He was away from De Wallen but not that far if he had to return in a hurry.

He found what he was looking for at the junction of Singel and Koningsplien. A cheap looking, no thrills hotel. The word 'vacancies' was displayed in the window by the entrance. The good thing was that it wasn't a big chain hotel. It looked like a small family owned and run establishment.

He entered, went to the reception counter, spoke to a middle-aged woman and sure enough they had a single for the night that would cost him seventy-five Euros. At this time of the year hotel rooms were not even a third of the price you would expect to pay in the high season. He was given the key to a room on the first floor overlooking the street.

The room was tidy. The bed had been made. The white crisp sheets were turned over, the pillow was puffed up. There was a fresh supply of coffee and milk in the do-it-yourself kit.

Once in his room he quickly unpacked his bag with his belongings. Then he took Kiri's bag, opened it and emptied the contents on the bed. He recalled how Petters had asked him about her bag. It was a strange request at the time. Why was he so interested in the bag? He couldn't care less about her being snatched off the street. He was more concerned about the bag.

The bag looked new, hardly used. There were a couple of tops, a bra and pants set. A pair of stone-washed denim jeans. A bomber jacket with a fur lined collar. A pair of weather beaten training shoes. A make-up bag full of mascara, creams, and a pair of eyebrow tweezers. A small spangled purse containing some jewellery: trinkets, bangles, bracelets, finger rings. There was also an item of female hygiene. He searched through the garments. Looking in the pockets of the jeans and the jacket. He found nothing but for a few coins, a cheap cigarette lighter, a used tram ticket, an open packet of cigarette papers and a pouch of rolling tobacco.

He looked under a cardboard base. Nothing. There was nothing else in the bag. Definitely no obvious evidence of drugs or anything else. There were two small pockets on the end. He opened them. They were empty. He shook the bag. He thought he felt something move. The bag did seem slightly heavier than it should have been.

He turned the bag over and examined the stitching along the seams. He may have been mistaken, but it looked as if some of the stitching was a slightly different shade and thickness to the rest of it. He laid the bag flat on the bed and ran the palm of his hand over it. There was something lodged in the lining, a bulge like shape, inserted into the lining. When he ran his hand over it he could feel it. It was evident to the touch. The stitching looked slightly ragged as if it had been picked open, then re-sewn by hand and not by a machine. He had to cut the stitching. He looked around for something with a sharp point then remembered the tweezers in her make-up bag. He opened the bag and extracted the tweezers.

He cut the stitching, unpicked it then pulled at it. The thread was fairly tight, nevertheless it soon came free. Once it was wide enough he slipped his fingers inside and hey-pesto. He could feel a small silk purse inserted into the gap between the bottom of the bag and one of the side pockets. He got hold of the silk bag and pulled it free. Inside there was something wrapped in tinfoil. He unwrapped the tinfoil and put it to one side. The foil may have been used to prevent the package being detected by an X-ray machine. It had been used to conceal an envelope. Grey-white in colour. Fairly thick. It was neatly folded along creased lines. It was only say ten centimetres square at most. He placed it onto the bed and looked at it. Now he knew where he had seen such a small envelope before. It was one couriers used to carry diamonds. He opened the end, turned it upside down and let the contents fall onto his palm.

'Oh my word,' he said to himself as a cascade of diamonds spilled out onto his palm. In the light they twinkled like stars. He was far from being an authority or expert on diamonds. Nevertheless, they looked like the real thing. There must have been about forty; no make that fifty diamonds. All of them about half a centimetre in diameter. He examined them. They were not bigger than a cheap ear stud. He didn't know if they were rough-cut or whatever. All he knew was that they were diamonds. That is why Petters was so interested in the bag. He knew what it contained. Were they using Kiri to smuggle diamonds into the UK? Then the penny dropped for he recalled that Amsterdam was Europe's foremost diamond centre. 'Geez,' he said to himself. He carefully opened the envelope and poured the merchandise back into the folds of paper. He placed the envelope deep into his trouser pocket.

The hotel was small and no thrills, but what it lacked in amenities it made up for in comfort. In a ground floor room there was a single PC which the guests could use free of charge to access the Internet.

At around six in the evening Kilbane went downstairs to the room. He logged on and for the next fifteen minutes he searched for everything and anything about diamonds. It didn't tell him a great deal, but when he typed, 'diamonds+Amsterdam' into the search engine, it opened up a whole new perspective. He instantly discovered that, just six weeks ago, there had been a raid on a diamond distribution facility not a million miles from here. An English language report from a local news agency said that several hundred, police estimated, as many as seven hundred rough cut diamonds had been stolen in the raid. The value of the heist was said to be around three and a half million Euros or two million, five hundred thousand pounds sterling at today's exchange rate. Kilbane estimated that he had the best part of two hundred thousand pounds worth of rough-cut stones in his pocket. Police had no leads at this time. Kilbane would give anyone very short odds that is where the diamonds had come from.

That got him thinking. The stolen diamond trade wasn't Arron Bron's scene. There was no way a runt like him would be involved in anything as big as this. He was a loan shark and a bully. Smuggling diamonds was way-out of his league. It occurred to Kilbane that Bron was acting as a go-between. His job was to deliver the girl to someone in London. He wouldn't know that she was carrying diamonds. Kilbane doubted that Kiri knew the diamonds were in the bag.

It was now seven-thirty in the evening. Outside behind the closed net curtains over the window it was dark. Kilbane was sitting in a chair by the side of the bed, waiting for a phone call from Eric Petters or Peter DeGroot.

He doubted if the call would ever come. The overhead light was out so the room was in dark. He was contemplating his next move. Outside the rush-hour had melted away and there was little sound of activity. There wasn't much traffic on the street below. He thought that the hotel was mostly unoccupied as he had not heard other guests on the creaking staircase. Then he recalled that when he had checked-in most of the keys to the other dozen, or so, rooms were dangling there on hooks. There wasn't a lot of demand for hotel rooms in the first week of December.

It was a few minutes before he was altered to a sound. It was a sound he had heard before when he came up the stairs. The sound of creaking floorboards. He listened and sure enough there was a creak as if someone was on the landing outside his room, stealthily stepping by the door. The sound was intermittent. It wasn't a natural movement. The sound would stop then the person would take another step as if he or she was walking on raised tiptoes. He strained his ears. Then the shock of all shocks, the sound of someone inserting something into the keyhole on the other side of the door. He could hear metal on metal as if a key was being inserted into the keyhole.

He quickly, but carefully got out of the chair and stepped to the other side of the door frame. Within a second, the bolt came open, then the door opened to a narrow degree. The light on the landing came into the room illuminating the floor with its glow. Whoever it was must have assumed the room was vacant. A hand appeared inside and reached for the light switch. The hand contained a black revolver. Kilbane felt his throat go as dry as a bone and his heart beat race at ten to the dozen. He chanced a glance around the door frame then automatically clenched his fists. The lower part of the intruder's arm was now in the room. In an instant Kilbane stepped back a pace, raised his foot and slammed it against the door. The solid edge flew back, trapping the arm against the door frame. The person let out a blood curding scream, then dropped the gun to the floor so it hit the bare boards with a solid thud.

    Kilbane rammed his shoulder against the door and pushed on it with all his might. The intruder let out another scream. The edge of the door pressing onto his arm would snap it with ease. Kilbane stepped forward, released the force on the door, then he grabbed the intruders arm, took his weight, and threw the intruder into the room, turning him over his shoulder in a classic Judo throw. The intruder fell to the floor with an almighty thump. He was in such a position that the upper half of his body was resting against the edge of the bedframe. Kilbane aimed a kick and smashed it into his face. Knocking him over in the process and onto the edge of consciousness. Kilbane scoped down to retrieve the handgun, then reached up to turn on the overhead light. The man before him wasn't a total stranger. It was the man who had witnessed Kiri being snatched. The very same man who had given him the car registration number. Now, he wasn't wearing the black frame spectacles.

    There was blood in his mouth, escaping through the gaps in-between his teeth. Kilbane leant over him, took a tight hold of his jacket lapels and shook him like a rag doll. The man's left arm sat limp. Kilbane couldn't resist it. He let go off him, raised his foot and stamped it on the exposed arm with all his might. The man may have come to kill him. He let out another yelp of pain. Kilbane grasped him by his hair and pulled his head upright. He looked into his eyes.

"Where's the girl?" he asked.

The man didn't reply so he delivered a clenched fist to his right shoulder that instantly dislocated his collar bone. "Where's the girl?" he asked again and poised his hand over the other shoulder.

"In a club," the man said breathlessly.

"Which club?" Kilbane asked.

"The Bird-Cage," he replied

"Where is it?"

"On the main canal. In Wallen."

Kilbane opened the man's jacket, dipped a hand into an inside jacket and pulled out a wallet which was thick with Euro banknotes. He slipped the wallet into his own back pocket.

"Come on. Take me," said Kilbane. He placed the handgun inside the belt of his trousers. It felt like a solid piece of metal.

"Is it loaded?" he asked.

The man didn't reply.

"Get on your feet," Kilbane ordered.

He stepped back a few paces and watched the man force himself up and get onto his feet. The blood emerging from his mouth was thick and frothy. He wasn't a big man but neither was he small. It was just that he had picked a fight with the wrong guy. He was wearing a light jacket over a striped sports type of casual shirt. Neat two-tone trousers. Shiny brown brogues on his feet. He didn't look like an assassin. Maybe that was his cover. This is what real assassins look like. Ordinary looking blokes, dressed in ordinary clothes so they blend into the background and don't look out of place. Maybe he had come to find the diamonds, not to kill him, but why carry a gun? He had shown his intention. Kilbane wouldn't drop his guide; despite the fact that the man's lower arm may have been broken and his shoulder dislocated it didn't mean that he wouldn't try to attack him. Kilbane laid down the house rules.

"I want you to take me to the club. If you run, I swear I'll kill you." He meant every word.

The man didn't utter a response. He got to his feet. He held his right hand high across his chest as if it hurt him bad. He groaned and winced with the strain. His face portrayed real pain. Kilbane wasn't about to be hoodwinked by smart acting. He stood a couple of feet back from him and watched him closely.

"Lead the way," he ordered. The man stepped out of the room and onto the landing. Kilbane stayed several feet behind him. They descended the stairs to the reception area. The hotel manager, a buxom big busted middle-aged lady, watched in stunned silence as they came down the stairs. She could see that the man leading the way was bleeding from a wound to his mouth. By the way he was holding his arm it was clear to see that he was having difficulty holding it up. She must have been aware of something happening in the room by the thuds that had come from above.

As they stepped by the reception counter Kilbane made eye contact with her.

"Contact the police," he advised. "I'll be back soon to explain." She looked at him with an expression that enforced the stunned silence she displayed. He dipped a hand into his trouser pocket, extracted the silk purse holding the diamonds and deposited it on the counter top.

"Look after these," he asked. Her mouth opened, and a faint gasp came out. She took the telephone and lifted it out of the cradle. Kilbane kept a tight grip on the handgun in his jacket pocket. He followed the man out of the door and into the night.

CHAPTER 7

Once outside of the hotel they ventured along Singel. The evening air was chilly. A thin layer of white mist was levitating above the water in the canal. Kilbane sucked in a breath of air that burned in his lungs. The sky was clear, so the light of a full moon was free to reflect on the heads of the cobble stones, and in the flat smooth surface of the canal. The man led the way onto Rokin and on towards De Wallen. Kilbane stayed two paces behind him. There wasn't a great deal of activity on the street. The traffic was sparse. A half empty tram came rattling by. Its inner lights bright, the sounds of the wheels against the rails made a loud grate. The stores along Rokin were open, though trade looked to be quiet. Kilbane lifted the collar of his jacket to his face. The cold night air penetrated deep into his bones. He kept his eyes on the man. They didn't say a word to each other. The man led the way along the path and they soon made it into Dam Square, then down a side street and into De Wallen. The number of people sauntering through the area had increased several-fold. They passed groups of tourists taking photographs. The cafes and restaurants were just starting to get busy, the smells and sounds of the entertainment area were all around.

As they came to the junction of Dam and the first canal, Kilbane stepped close to the man. "Where's the place?" he asked.

"Just along here," he replied. He had an English accent that Kilbane couldn't place. He pointed in the direction to take.

"You lead the way. Don't try anything," Kilbane warned. The guy winced.

They came out of the street to the first canal. They stepped towards the hump back bridge over the canal. There was activity along the side of the canal in the bars and clubs, cafes, and other establishments. Flashing neon lights and vice. The area wasn't at its busiest but there were a few people about.

As they reached the top of the bridge, Kilbane saw his opportunity and he didn't flinch. He forced the man to the side of the railing. Brutal as it was he barged him with all his might, hitting him in his upper back with a combination of his elbow and arm. The force propelled him over the top railing. He tried to stop himself from going over, but he couldn't hold onto the rail or stop his own momentum. He let out a cry as he somersaulted over the railing and crashed head-first into the water twenty feet below. He made an all mighty splash as he went under. The sound was partially hidden under the noise from all around. But someone on the canal side had seen the man fall into the canal and instantly let out a shout which alerted several people nearby. They rushed to the edge of the canal to see what had happened. Kilbane kept on walking. He didn't turn his head to look back. If anyone had seen him do it, they didn't appear to be keen to tackle him or ask him why. The passers-by were more concerned with the wellbeing of the person who had fallen into the water.

Kilbane carried on over the bridge. At the bottom he turned right, along the side of the canal and ventured onward in a calm walk. Further ahead in the near distance he could make out the neon lights of a club and the mock-up of an exotic bird in a metal bird cage hanging from the façade of the building. He had arrived at the Bird-Cage Lap-dancing club.

There was a small group of people standing outside of the entrance. A doorman in a dark ankle length coat was by the door. It was his job to entice the passers-by to come in with a few choice words of encouragement. He and another man were looking back along the canal at the activity near to the bridge. Clearly the news that someone had fallen into the canal had filtered down the street. Kilbane remained calm and in control. He stepped into the splash of light at the entrance. Photographs of the half-naked girls who performed in the club were placed in glass frames. The usual blurb, accompanied the photographs. It said. 'Best pole dancing club in Amsterdam'.

The guy in the long coat looked at Kilbane. "What happened up there?" he asked in English.

Kilbane glanced back. "I think someone fell into the canal. He must be drunk and staggered in."

The guy shook his head. He could see that Kilbane was wondering whether to enter the club. Suddenly the pull of a potential paying customer brought his attention back to his job.

"Thirty Euro entrance. Nice girls and pole dancing," he said.

"Thirty?" replied Kilbane. He made his intention known by stepping through the half open door and into the bright interior where he was met by a pay window. He took out the wad of notes in his pocket, peeled off the required entrance fee, paid at the window and stepped into the Bird-Cage. He was relieved to be off the street and out of view; because no doubt the police would soon be on the scene asking for witnesses.

Inside, the lights were low. The lighting scheme was a shade of crimson red. The place was hot in every sense of the word. Girls in various stages of undress were performing around metal poles placed on a raised stage that dissected the floor into four quarters. Some were spinning. Others holding on. There was a lot of flesh on display.

It was a classy type of place; not your run-down strip joint. It was all lace and silk and dark walls festooned with black and white prints of long legged models and nudes in a contemporary style. A quick techno beat was belting out a rhythm for the performers to gyrate to. The open floor space was quite a large area. It was much more spacious than any similar establishment he had been into in London. Girls were performing on a raised stage that ran along the length of the floor, then across so it was split into a + shape. At each end of the four catwalks was a circular stage. Some of the performers were already naked; others were wearing long gowns that would shortly be discarded. Metal poles were placed at intervals along the four stages. Girls were twirling around them like crazy spinning tops. Others were gyrating up and down the poles in the most sensual way possible. Never let it be said that pole dancing wasn't artistic. There was a cross selection of performers of all shapes and sizes, colours, and creeds. It was nothing if not a multi-cultural strip show.

CHAPTER 8

Kilbane ventured forward into the middle of the floor. There were a few customers sitting at tables close to the stage. The only females were those on stage or those wearing skimpy bikinis and working as waitresses. A bar counter was along the back wall.

Kilbane sat at a table by the end of the stage. Above him a girl, who had only a negligee and thong for company, was dancing around a pole. Once settled he looked around to get his bearings. The corners were in shadow, but he could see that the audience was made up by a combination of middle aged men in suits, guys on a lad's night out and the lone wolf male. A couple of men in tuxedos and bow ties were patrolling the floor to ensure that none of the customers got too close to the performers.

If the truth be told Kilbane was impressed. It was quite tasteful in most respects. The real action would be in the private booths were anything would go, particularly the money in the punters' pockets. If anyone wanted a close and personal dance, then it would cost a lot more than the thirty Euro entrance fee.

Within thirty seconds of sitting down one of the waitresses waltzed up to the table. She was a short, wiry framed girl of east Asia appearance. Long dark hair that shimmered around her shoulder blades. She had a nice, cute smile and a firm body. She was carrying a silver tray. She looked at Kilbane and caught his eye. The scent of a perfume was evidence. She said something he didn't quite catch under the blare of the music. He looked into her eyes.

"Do you speak English?" he asked.

"You like beer?"

He asked for a bottle of beer, any kind, and demonstrated the size of the bottle with his hands. She turned away from him. He watched her move across the floor, go up a step and into bar area. She gave the order to one of the two barmen behind the bar. Along the wall from the bar was an arched exit with the words, 'The Fantasy Room', etched around the edge. A girl, one of the performers, was taking a guy through the arch. It probably led to the private dance rooms were the punter would receive some one-on-one action, in the form of oral sex. Girl on boy.

He observed the dancer on the stage above him. She had propelled herself upside down on the pole so everything was hanging loose; her hair was touching the surface. Her flimsy gown had dropped so she was displaying a dark thong wedged between her long shapely legs. The platform shoes on her feet where nearly touching the ceiling.

The waitress returned to the table with a small bottle of beer and a glass on the tray. "That is ten Euro," she requested.

Kilbane took the roll of banknotes for his pocket and let her see the thickness of the wad. He looked into her face then glanced around in a wide sweep. "Tell me. Do you know a girl called Kiri?" he asked.

She didn't seem to understand him. She screwed her face into a questioning expression. "What you say?" She stepped closer to him.

Kilbane peeled off a twenty Euro note from the wad and placed it onto the tray. He maintained eye contact with her. "I'm looking for a girl called Kiri. K.I.R.I. An English girl. Do you know her?" He took the bottle of beer and the glass off the tray.

She didn't reply immediately. It was as if she was trying to decipher his words. After all he spoke with an accent that may have been difficult for her to understand. It took her a few seconds to respond.

She shook her head. "No one I know." she replied but she didn't sound convincing. Maybe she did know someone of that name but was scared to admit it. Kilbane maintained eye contact with her.

"I will pay." He peeled off another twenty euro note which he placed on the tray. "For you. For any information," he said.

She took one of the twenties and placed it inside the cup of her bikini top. "I bring some money," she said.

Kilbane watched her go to the bar and speak with the bartender. Then she made her way back to the table but took a different route in order to speak to a tall, older woman in a long sparkling gown who was obviously one of the performers or the floor manager. Kilbane saw her whisper something into her ear. The oriental girl pointed towards Kilbane. The woman turned her head to look in Kilbane's direction. Obviously, the waitress had told her something about the English guy sitting at the table over there. The conversation did not last more than a few seconds before the Asian girl made her way to Kilbane with his change. She looked at him as she handed him a ten Euro note but moved away from him without saying a word. As she moved away the tall blonde woman in the long gown glided to the table. She was tall and chubby. Now that she was nearer he could see that she was somewhere in the late forties to early fifties age range. The gown was loose around her midriff and split open down the middle. The curves of her boobs were squashed together through the opening. Her hair was long and up in a kind of seventies beehive style. She had a blunt feminine look. She eyed Kilbane closely. He noticed the fancy rings on her fingers. One was a huge imitation opal stone. The other had a shell-like design.

"Would Sir like to see Kiri?" she asked in a voice that had a Germanic edge. She had the hint of a grin on her face.

"Yes. I would," he replied.

She remained serious. "An excellent choice. Follow me." She turned her back on him and began to move across towards the bar area. He got up out of the seat, followed her up a short flight of steps and onto the floor space in front of the bar. He didn't know what was about to happen, whether she was going to take him to Kiri or whether there was some other purpose to all this or if there was another performer called Kiri. He felt the gun in his jacket pocket.

The madam took him towards the arch with the words, 'Fantasy Room', circled around it. On the way he clapped eyes on a man in a tuxedo who gave him a fleeting glance. He followed the madam into the archway. It led into a corridor. Directly ahead there was a dead end. To the right was a door marked 'Private' and one to the left that went behind the bar. The overhead lighting was misty red, so it had an edgy, almost psychedelic ambience.

There were a set of rooms along the corridor with flimsy curtains across the openings. These were the private dance rooms. The curtains over the first two rooms were closed. The sound of a moan escaped from one of the rooms. Perhaps the customer was receiving more than a private dance. The madam stepped down the corridor to the second set of curtains. She turned into the second cubicle on the left, opened the curtain, and took him into the space.

"Come in and we can discuss terms. Kiri will be with you in a moment."

As he stepped into the room the madam closed the curtain behind him. The room was only around ten feet square at most. There was a round back, upholstered chair where the punter sat to receive his private dance. It had a thin carpet on the floor and plain painted side panel walls.

The Madam smiled. "Kiri costs a lot. She is one of our most popular girls. It is five hundred Euro for oral sex." She was very matter of fact. Her accent was either German, Polish or Ukrainian.

Kilbane extracted the roll of banknotes from his pocket, counted out five one hundred Euro notes and handed them to the madam.

"Kiri will be with you in a moment. Please make yourself comfortable." He did as told and sat down in the armchair. The madam closed the curtain over the opening. The moans from the next room became ones of climatic excitement. Kilbane waited in anticipation.

A long minute passed before there was a sound of movement in the corridor. The madam entered the room followed, a few paces behind her, by a girl in a Baby-Doll negligee. The madam introduced her to the customer.

"This is Karina," she said.

Kilbane looked up from his seat and clapped his eyes on the model. It wasn't Kiri. This girl was at least five years older and five inches taller. She was wearing a see-through negligée with a skimpy string bra and string thong underneath. A head of straight auburn dyed hair fell down her back. In the light her skin was the shade of milky coffee. Make-up had been applied to her eyes and face. She looked, for all the world, like a voyeur's wet dream.

The madam glanced at her then at the paying customer. "This is your date. I trust you will be satisfied."

"Sure," said Kilbane. As if he was highly enthusiastic about what was to come.

"You have twenty minutes together." She tried to say with a smile, but even she couldn't pull it off. Kilbane said nothing.

As she departed she pulled the thick curtain across the opening. They were alone. Kilbane felt deflated. Nevertheless, he was still determined to locate Kiri. He looked at the girl then got to his feet. She was about to fall onto her knees.

"No. No. I don't want anything like that," he protested.

Karina looked at him with an expression of puzzlement. "What you want? Fucky-fucky?" Her English contained a heavy Asian accent. She was either Vietnamese or from somewhere in that ball-park.

"No. No sex. I'm looking for another girl." She looked put out. As if he didn't find her attractive or something. "No, it's not like that. I need to try and find Kiri. Kiri Porter, an English girl. Do you know her?"

The twitch in her eye said she did.

"Where is she?" he asked.

"I not know," she replied.

"Does she work here?"

"Yes. She work here."

At least Kilbane had confirmation. "I need to find her. Where is she?"

"Maybe she is in room."

"Which room?"

"Downstair."

"Where is it?"

"It this way."

"Will you help me find her? I need to find her. She's in danger. Do you understand?"

"I understand."

"Please can you show me to the room?" he asked.

She stalled to think about it, then looked back as if she suspected they were being observed. "Okay. I help you."

She went to the curtain, opened it, and peered out onto the corridor. The way was clear. She turned to him. "This way."

She stepped through the curtain and led him onto the corridor where she turned left and headed towards the door marked: 'Private'.

The thud of the music from the dance floor was incessant. He could hardly hear himself think. He followed her to the door. She took the handle and opened it. It led straight into the dancer's dressing room. The illumination was bright. It was like something out of the 'Showgirls' movie. On the back wall was a continuous line of mirrors with light bulbs along the top edge. Several of the girls were standing in front of the mirrors applying make-up. Several were half naked, others were dressed in robes. The smell of make-up and perfume was almost overpowering. Clothing was hanging over the backs of chairs and scattered on the floor. One girl was using a hairdryer. One had rollers in her hair. As Kilbane entered one of the girls turned to face them. She gave him a kind of wave then carried on applying false lashes to her eyes. It would appear that it wasn't uncommon for men to come in here.

Karina turned to the left and headed to a closed door just a couple of yards further ahead. She opened the door inward. It revealed a dark corridor with a short flight of wooden steps going down ten feet or so into a basement. It was dingy, damp and smelled fusty. The light from the changing room just about penetrated to the bottom of the steps to reveal a bare stone floor then nothing but shadow. Before taking the steps, she turned to Kilbane. She seemed reluctant to go down the steps. Maybe it was because she didn't know what she would discover or perhaps she was fearful of the dark. Kilbane moved passed her. He ran his hand along the wall to feel for a light switch. He found one and switched a light on. A single bulb in the ceiling illuminated the passageway. He could see a closed door on the right-hand side. He descended the wooden steps running his hand along the bannister for support.

Down he went, one step at a time. The weight of the gun in the pocket sagged his jacket to one side. He took a few steps then came to the door. He tried the handle and pushed on it. The door was locked, but not particularly solid. Nothing much more than half-inch thick ply board. The round knob handle was rickety. The door was loose. He could see a thin pencil beam of light inside. He knocked on the door.

"Kiri, are you in there?" he asked in a raised voice, then listened for a response but didn't get one. He looked to the top of the stairs to see that the girl in the baby-doll nightwear silhouetted against the light. A second girl had joined her. The sound of the hairdryer had ceased. It was quiet in the dressing room, though the thump-thump-thump of the music on the dance floor was still a reminder of where he was.

He tried the door again. There was only one thing for it. He stepped back a couple of paces until his back was against the wall, then he raised his foot. With every ounce of strength in his body he kicked at the door at a point just above the handle. The force smashed the door. The lock bolt mechanism held. He took another step back and again kicked at the frame for a second time. The bolt snapped. The door shuddered and bounced wide open.

He stepped inside and immediately clapped eyes on Kiri. She was laid on a mattress on a stone floor in a foetal position. It was a store room of some description as there were a few fixtures and fittings with what looked like a section of stage, an amplifier and a couple of other miscellaneous items, including a roll of curtain.

Kiri was wearing the same clothes he had last seen her in. She raised her head and saw Kilbane in the doorway.

"Come on," he encouraged. "We're getting out of here."

She didn't move. It was as if she was sleepy from the effect of drink or drugs or both. She seemed zonked out on something. Her eyes looked vacant and distant. Her movements were slow and laborious. She was almost zombie like.

"For fuck sake. What have the bastards done to you?" he asked.

He reached down, grabbed her and managed to pull her up onto her feet. He grasped her hand and pulled her towards the door and out onto the corridor. There were now several girls in the doorway looking down the steps. Kilbane didn't saunter he hauled Kiri up the stairs. In the dressing room two of the girls were still standing at the mirror preening themselves. As Kilbane and Kiri came into the room they turned to look at them. One of them could only gawp with open mouthed shock on her face. Kilbane didn't care to explain what was going on. He held Kiri up and escorted her out of the room and into the red crimson haze of the corridor leading to the private dance rooms.

Just as they neared the junction with the corridor leading to the private rooms the madam appeared. The expression on her face was a picture of combined shock and stunned surprise. She looked at Kiri, then motioned her mouth as if she was about to say something. Kilbane didn't want her to say a word.

"Shut it," he shouted. Then as if he needed to enforce that he was in charge he yanked the gun out of his jacket, raised it and pointed it at her forehead from a distance of no more than a few feet. His finger was poised on the trigger. One wrong move and he would blow her to kingdom come.

She froze on the spot. As she came into range he couldn't help but swing his hand towards her. The butt end of the gun smashed into her mouth, dislodging several front row teeth. The force of the blow sent her spiralling back into the curtain. As she lost balance and fell over she instinctively grabbed hold of the curtain. In doing so she pulled it off the rail and the connectors popped one-by-one as they slid off the track. She went to the ground with the curtain not far behind her. Behind in the room, a small dark-skinned girl appeared and saw the madam sprawled out on the floor and the gun in Kilbane's hand. She let out a loud piercing shriek thereby alerting anyone within earshot. Kilbane reacted by reaching back to grab Kiri's arms. He pulled her towards him and they stepped through the arch and out onto the floor adjacent to the bar counter.

The music was so loud it was highly unlikely that any of the punters or the staff were aware of anything untoward. But in the next moment Kilbane was aware that one of the barmen was just coming around the counter to the right. His body was set in an aggressive stance. Kilbane had little option but to raise the gun and point it at him. The fellow stopped dead in his tracks and lifted his hands above his head. Kilbane looked to his side to see a fire alarm button imbedded into the wall about five feet away from him. He hastily went to it and rammed the butt end of the gun into the glass cover. The force penetrated deep into the device and instantly set the alarm ringing. Within five seconds of hitting the alarm the house lights had come on and the music had stopped.

It took the punters and the performers another three to four seconds to react to the sound of the alarm sounding. Then everything stopped. A loud internal alarm was sounding with an eardrum splitting 'blur-blur-blur'. Kilbane edged forward. He saw his chance to create panic.

"Fire," he shouted at the top of his voice. One of the performers screamed. Then there was a stampede of Lazarus proportions as those on the floor scattered in the direction of the main exit. More screams and general panic ensued. People were emerging from the darkened corners. The young guys who had been acting like cool dudes with the girls were now showing their true colours and vaulting towards the exit. The dancers were grabbing what they could and were legging it across the stage towards the main exit. It was a mad scene. One of sheer panic. It was what people have been programmed to do on the sound of an alarm.

Kilbane took Kiri by the arm, tugged her and like the rest of the patrons and performers they made a bee line to the exit. "Get out fire," he shouted again.

Tables and chairs were knocked over in the rush to escape. The doors leading into the area around the pay window and the exit had been forced wide open. A wave of petrified people were disappearing through the exit and out onto the darkened street by the side of the canal. The place was emptied in ten seconds flat. It was everyone for themselves. It was panic mode.

As they emerged out into the open by the canal side Kilbane, who was still holding Kiri upright, was able to fight his way through the crowd. The fresh air was welcoming. The sky overhead was clear, the moonlight reflecting in the rippling waters of the canal. It was only then that he realised that Kiri didn't have anything on her feet. He had to sweep her up into his arms. She didn't resist, nor did she say anything. She was still zonked out. They were quickly lost in the crowd who were now milling around the outside of the club and spread out across narrow street to the edge of the canal.

CHAPTER 9

Kilbane maintained a firm hold of Kiri. She couldn't have weighed more than one hundred and twenty pounds. He could taste her scent in his nostrils and feel her hair on his face. She was nothing but a bundle of skin and bones in his arms.

Near to the bridge, there was some emergency services activity. The blue and white lights of a police car or an ambulance, or both, were sweeping along the facades of the canal side buildings like some spinning neon searchlight. They were looking for the man who had fallen into the canal, or maybe he was in the ambulance or in the back of the police car. Maybe he had drowned. Kilbane didn't much care. He had Kiri in his arms. Her hair was blowing up into his face. She moaned. Some people who were gathered around the emergency vehicles glanced at them but didn't say a word. Maybe the girl was drunk or overcome with panic.

As soon as they made it to Dam Square, they joined a small queue in a taxi rank outside of the Krasnapolsky Hotel. It took a few minutes for them to reach the summit of the line. Once in a taxi they travelled the short distance to the hotel on Koningsplien.

Kilbane led Kiri through the door into the hotel reception. There was no evidence that the police were or had been there. A clock above the reception counter said ten after eleven. The manageress behind the counter had been joined by a male in a similar age range to her. As Kilbane and Kiri entered they looked at them in silence. The look of shock and concern on their faces. Kilbane felt jiggered though his arms had just about recovered from carrying her. He tried to put them at ease by smiling, but it didn't work. He put Kiri down onto a bench opposite the counter. The man could only ogle with a slack jawed gape. Kilbane looked at them.

"Can you get her a blanket and a warm drink?" he asked. "Make it a brandy. She's frozen stiff." The woman looked at the man and said something in Dutch. He immediately did as she asked.

Kilbane stepped to the counter, slipped his hand into the hem of his belt, and withdrew the handgun. On seeing the weapon, she took a step back. He gently placed the weapon on the counter top. She stared at the gun then at him. Her eyes were wide, but she didn't appear to be frightened. She was cool or maybe she was trying to act cool. Maybe inside she was shaking like a leaf.

"Look after that will you?" he asked.

"The police have been," she said.

"Good. Call them again will you."

She put in a second call to the police.

The man soon returned with a blanket and a glass containing what looked like a healthy tot of Brandy. He gave the glass to Kilbane. He encouraged Kiri to drink the liquor but not to take it in one gulp, only to sip it. He placed the blanket around her shoulders. She looked up at him and smiled at him for the first time. They waited in silence for the police to return.

It was twenty past eleven when a police car arrived outside of the hotel. Two uniformed officers from the local constabulary entered and came into the reception area. One was female. The other male. The male officer took the lead at the counter while the female observed Kilbane and Kiri on the bench. He was a tall, fair-haired guy, handsome looking and immaculate in his police uniform. He kept his hand poised in his holster where his regulation firearm was located. He spoke to the manager and her partner in Dutch. He didn't seem to be too concerned when the woman handed him a handgun. He looked at Kilbane. Kilbane didn't know what was being said. They could have been talking about anything for all he knew. He kept his arm around Kiri and his backside on the bench. He glanced at the female officer and smiled at her. She was a pretty lady in her early thirties or so. She did respond to his smile by gently nodding her head, but she remained stony faced, business like and kept her eyes on them. A radio communication device attached to the belt around her waist crackled. A metallic radio voice said a few words. She responded by taking the device off her belt and speaking into the unit.

After thirty seconds or so the male officer approached Kilbane. He kept his hands close to his utility belt, but he could sense from experience that he had little to fear from Kilbane.

"What are your names?" he asked in English.

"David Kilbane and Kiri Porter."

"Where did you get the firearm?"

Kilbane stayed focused on his eyes. "I took it off a man who came here to kill me."

"Where is the man?" he asked.

"At the bottom of a canal."

The officer's face didn't crack. Just then his radio unit came to life. He heard a command. He responded, only saying a few words, then he regained eye contact with Kilbane.

"We are taking you two to police headquarters. You can explain everything there."

"Did you get the diamonds?" asked Kilbane.

"Yes. We got the diamonds," he replied.

"Good. At least you know I'm on the level."

The police officers said nothing, but they understood what he was saying.

Kilbane and Kiri were escorted to the waiting police car and driven the relatively short distance to the main Amsterdam police headquarters on Elandsgracht in Jordaan.

CHAPTER 10

The central Amsterdam Police headquarters was a brick and window building probably dating from the late 1950's or the early 1960's. It was nothing if bland. Four floors high. Not a massive building by any stretch of the imagination. Like anything you would find in any major British city.

The car stopped outside of the main entrance. Kilbane and Kiri, who was still wrapped in the blanket were shown inside by the two officers.

It was in every sense of the word a conventional police station with an entrance area and counter where a team of three uniformed officers were dealing with anyone requiring to be booked in and processed. At eleven-thirty on a crisp, chilly, frost laden December night there wasn't a lot going on. Once inside the building Kilbane and Kiri were asked to sit on a bench opposite the counter and wait. The male officer approached the counter and spoke to his colleague who tapped in the details into a computer monitor. The usual banal stuff. Nothing exciting. The female officer disappeared for a couple of minutes then returned carrying an overcoat which she handed to Kiri.

Kiri seemed to be coming around to her senses. Whatever they had given her in the, 'Bird-Cage', seemed to be wearing off. Maybe it was the nip of brandy she had drunk or the cold night air; but she seemed to be responding and regaining some of her senses.

It was another ten minutes before there was any kind of a development. The procedures of police matters can run slowly. What happened next didn't surprise Kilbane. First, he and Kiri were separated. Kiri was taken off to be seen by a female doctor. Watching her being led away, down a corridor and through a door was the last time Kilbane ever clapped eyes on Kiri Porter. As soon as she was gone, he was taken into the bowels of the building and into an interview room. He was escorted by three uniformed officers along a corridor, down some stairs and into an interview room.

The room contained a single table, several chairs, and an audio recording machine. He had had some brushes with the police back home, so it wasn't as if he wasn't experienced in such matters. He handled it well, after all he had nothing much to worry about.

Once in the room he sat at the table. The room was windowless and featureless. The walls were a drab splash of grey. The floor a patchwork of plain black and white tiles. A radiator was belching out a warm air that had the room as warm as toast.

It was another few minutes before two suits joined him and the uniformed officers. The two suits were detectives. Both looked like experienced guys. Both in their mid-to-late forties. One was average height, average features. The other was taller and far slicker with thick, dark wavy hair and nice features. They sat at the table opposite Kilbane. One of them produced a briefcase, which he laid on the table top and from which he extracted the handgun and the packet of diamonds, both in sealed, protective plastic zip-top evidence bags.

The interrogation soon commenced. They asked him a series of questions. Why was he in Amsterdam? Where did he get the handgun? All the questions you would expect. He told them everything from the word go. How he had been persuaded to travel to Amsterdam to collect a package. How he had met Peter DeGroot expecting to receive an envelope containing drugs, pills or whatever then how he had been totally stunned to discover that the package was a seventeen-year-old girl.

They were thorough with their questioning technique. One of them - the older guy would ask a question - Kilbane would answer it. Then the other one would ask him a supplementary question and try to blow a hole in his response and probe a weakness. They asked him where he had found the diamonds. He told them. One of the other uniformed officers was immediately despatched to the hotel to find the holdall and bring it back here for examination. They asked him how many diamonds there were in the envelope. Had he counted them? He said yes, he had. He counted forty. They asked him if he had any objection to being strip searched. He said no of course not. He had nothing to hide.

Instructions were issued in Dutch, no doubt concerning Peter DeGroot, Eric Petters and Hans VanBrooken. Little doubt that they would be receiving an early morning wake-up call in the next couple of hours.

After ninety minutes when the interview concluded Kilbane was charged with assault against the man he had attacked in the hotel. The very same man he had thrown into the canal. The man had been fished out of the canal. Barely alive, but still breathing. Kilbane said it was self-defence. He would do it again if he had to. They asked him if he wanted a lawyer. He declined the offer. Once again, he stated for the record that he had nothing to hide.

At the conclusion of the interrogation Kilbane was taken to the counter, formally arrested and charged with assault. He was then taken to the custody unit. At around one in the morning the uniformed officers carried out a strip search looking in the most intimate of places. They found nothing. He was taken to a cell.

The following morning, he was taken back to the interview room and there he was charged with assault against the madam in the, 'Bird-Cage', and for causing unnecessary panic. He laughed aloud.

CHAPTER 11

Kilbane was to remain in custody for the next forty-eight hours. On the third day a judge signed an order allowing the police to question him for a further thirty-six hours. He was transferred to a prison on the outskirts of Amsterdam where he was allowed a visit from a representative from the British Embassy. The chap told him they were working with the Dutch authorities to get this sorted out as quickly as possible.

Apparently, Kiri Porter had been returned to the UK. She had been taken by two members from the City of Manchester - Social Services Department - back home and reunited with her mother. She was a runaway from Manchester. Her mother hadn't seen her in two years. Kilbane was pleased to hear that she was back home, though he didn't know anything about her family.

The officer told Kilbane that the Dutch police were liaising with their colleagues in the Metropolitan Police. Aaron Bron and his crew had been taken in for questioning. Arrests were imminent

Kilbane spent another day on remand in a Dutch prison close to Schiphol airport. Then on the following day there was a major shift in tact and attitude. He was visited by the staff member from the British embassy who was accompanied by a member of the British National Crime Agency. Britain's equivalent to the FBI. Kilbane was informed that the Dutch police were willing to drop all charges against him. In fact, they wished to thank him for his role in solving the crime. Nearly all of the diamonds stolen in the Diamond Centre heist had been recovered. He had helped to bust a smuggling ring. He had also helped to bust the, 'Bird-Cage', who had been using underage girls as sex workers. What a sordid world we live in thought Kilbane. It gave him a sense of wellbeing that he had done something to make someone else's life a little better.

The guy he had thrown into the canal was named as a British man called Philip Mosley. He worked in the, Bird-Cage'. Hans VanBrooken the guy who was Eric Petters's right-hand man was one of the men who had snatched Kiri off the street.

Eric Petters had received one hundred diamonds from the heist. VanBrooken knew that Petters was using Kiri Porter to transport some of the diamonds to London for one of his British clients. But didn't know how. This was the reason VanBrooken and an associate abducted Kiri. They had taken her to the, 'Bird-Cage', and searched her for the diamonds. Only to discover that they were not hidden on her body. Then they assumed and rightly so, that they were in the holdall DeGroot had been given by Petters. Mosley discovered where Kilbane was staying. He tried to break into the room to find the holdall. He didn't know that Kilbane was in the room or that he was a Judo black belt who would kick his arse.

The chain was Petters, DeGroot, Bron then an end-buyer in London. Only Petters and the end-buyer knew that the diamonds were in the bag. Aaron Bron told Scotland Yard that he didn't know what the package was. Only that he had to deliver it to a man in Mayfair. Kilbane was right. Bron was only a middle man in the chain. Little more than a courier. Passing what he received from Amsterdam to a man in Mayfair for which he was going to be paid five thousand pounds. Bron said he had no idea who the end-buyer was.

Of course, there was a question about how many diamonds where in the envelope and how many Kilbane had handed over. When Petters was questioned he swore blind that he had placed fifty diamonds in the envelope. The envelope Kilbane had handed over only contained forty. Therefore, about fifty thousand pounds worth of diamonds were unaccounted for. Kilbane swore blind that there were only forty diamonds.

No one could ever be certain how many diamonds were in the envelope. Of course, Kilbane wasn't telling. Needless to say, he didn't admit where he had stashed the other ten diamonds, though he did plan a return trip to Amsterdam when the heat had died down. He was going to stay in the very same hotel and in the very same room for that his where he had hidden the diamonds.

They would stay hidden there until he had chance to return to retrieve them. He knew that he will be able to sell them on the black market for a decent sum. What he did with the money was another question. Whether or not he put it on gambling on the outcomes of football games. Maybe he had finally learnt his lesson. Gambling, every rarely, if ever pays off. It was a fool's game. He'd never seen a bookie on a bike. Trying to predict the outcomes of football games, was like the police trying to speculate on what had happened to the ten diamonds that hadn't been accounted for. Kilbane wasn't telling.

The End

The Returner

Chapter 1

There comes a time in everyone's life when death raises its ugly head. Like the passing of a loved one or a near death experience. I suppose it could be said to be part of the tapestry of life. Although, I had been feeling lethargic for a while I didn't think I was dying. It was probably because I had put on a few pounds in excess weight that I was feeling listless and out of breath.

The pain in my ribs, I put down to a strain of some kind and assumed it would pass. When it didn't I summoned up the courage to make an appointment to see my physician. My doctor, a chap called Peter Khan, took some of my blood and said he would get back in touch with me should there be a need to call me back. I didn't think I would hear from him again. When the test result came back Khan asked me to come and see him. I knew Dr Khan socially from the times we had met at our golf club. When I asked him to tell me straight and cut out the waffle he did so. It wasn't pleasant listening.

He told me that the blood test revealed that I had a blood disease that couldn't be cured. I had eight months to live. A year at the most.

I didn't like the idea of dying before my thirty-ninth birthday. Come to think of it I didn't like the idea of dying at all. I wasn't elderly. I was still in my prime. Needless, to say, when I received the diagnosis I was gob smacked, dumbstruck and mortified, all rolled into one. Who wouldn't be? I would also admit that I was fearful of the Grim Reaper. The only good point was that I appreciated Khan's frankness and candour. I had asked to be told. He told me!

He said that I would feel okay right up until the last month before my death, then I would go downhill at a rapid speed. As the disease took hold the final couple of weeks would be tough. It would be a battle but they would keep me as comfort as possible with a cocktail of drugs. It was a scenario that made me want to cry, but I manned up and put on a brave face.

Now that I knew I wouldn't be around in a year I had to think about the future. I had a wife, Claire, and two young children who had to be cared for. Alas, I wouldn't be able to complete any of the things on my bucket list; like driving along the California Pacific Coast Highway in a red Corvette with the roof open. I would never be able to do those things unless a miracle cure was found and a sudden windfall dropped out of the sky.

That got me thinking. To be honest I had been thinking about doing it for a long time. A get rich quick scheme. Circumstances meant that I would never do it, but now the goalposts had changed. I needed money. Now as the ramifications of impending death flowed through my mind I reconstructed the idea and raised it to a new level.

As I drove home from the surgery, in the north London traffic, I found myself thinking about the idea, once again. There were a few things I needed to do and someone to talk to. In all likelihood it wouldn't come off. But now I had little option but to take it a step further and determine if it might work. I had to provide for my wife and my two kids. My measly life insurance policy and a pittance of a pension wouldn't begin to pay for my children's education, never mind my wife's excesses. Consequently, any method to make a lot of money, easily and quickly was paramount.

That evening I arrived home at six o'clock. Claire may have been someone who spent money like it was going out of fashion, but she was a fabulous cook. She had prepared a gorgeous meal in her own inimitable style with expensive wine and the best truffle dessert. The children, my two boys, Jack aged ten and Ben six were in their bedroom playing on their X-box.

Claire and I had met when we enrolled onto the same Accountancy course at the University of Leeds. Whilst it wasn't love at first sight we quickly became friends and did the things first year students do, partying and generally having a good time. We dated a couple of times and went out with our friends. In the final year we shared a house in Headingly. After graduation we went our separate ways but kept in touch. I came back to my home in London. Claire, went home to Harrogate. Despite been parted by a couple of hundred miles we talked on the telephone every now and again. A year after university Claire secured a job in London, working for an auditing company in the City. I was a trainee investment broker for a small firm dealing with investment portfolios for a selective band of rich clients. We met up again. Claire came to live with me and my parents for a while, whilst she looked for a place of her own. We became lovers. When my parents were away I would take her into my bedroom and we would screw like a pair of alley cats for most of the afternoon. We eventually moved out of my parent's home into a two-up, two-down in Islington.

We were married four years later both at the age of twenty-four. That was fourteen years ago. Jack, our first-born, arrived in the summer four years later, followed by Ben four years after him. We were the perfect nuclear family with 2.65 children and a dog called Bruno. We had moved to our current home on a quiet road in Finchley, north London. We were happy and content. Despite the fact that I earned one hundred thousand pounds a year, rising to one hundred and fifty thousand with bonuses, we found it was never enough. We had a mortgage and all the usual debts like child-minding fees, expensive tastes, two top of the range cars and all the other vices.

I worked as tax and investment consultant for a small firm of investment brokers on the tenth floor of the Gherkin building in the City of London. Claire worked, every now and again, for a local estate agency.

My salary never covered Claire's excesses. I don't think she ever understood the cost of things. She seemed immune to the rising cost of living and the cost of things in general. Consequently, my salary was stretched to the limit to fund her whims. The problem was I loved her. She was the mother of my boys. Though my pay packet may have been more than the average Joe earned we were on the brink of a financial precipice. My wife's tastes in clothes, perfume, beauty parlour pampering, and holidays saw to that. Then there was the children's education to mull over during the sleepless nights I had to endure.

In order to keep things at home on an even keel I decided not to inform Claire that I would be dead in a year. The revelation would have been enough to send her into a tailspin of despair and panic. The shock alone might have been enough to kill her.

Chapter 2

I had first met the Oxton's five years ago. Derek Oxton was a self-made man who had made a boat-load of money in the iron and steel industry. He was a skilled and very shrewd asset stripper. He was a client of the firm I worked for. I had met him on several occasions to give him tax and investment advice. That was my forte. I had saved him hundreds of thousands of pounds in tax.

I didn't like him at all. Like a lot of rich people, he wasn't nice. He didn't have to be nice to anyone. The investment plan I managed for him was worth around ten million pounds. I had also created an investment portfolio for Mrs Oxton which was worth in excess of three million pounds. Their London home was on an exclusive millionaire's row of properties in a narrow slice of land in-between Hampstead to the west and Highgate to the east. The house was worth somewhere in the region of four million pounds. They also had homes in Florida, the Caribbean, and the south of France.

Old man Oxton was in his early seventies. Mrs Oxton was six years his junior. To be honest he was hard work, but she was a lovely caring lady, very chatty, warm and convivial. All told the Oxton's were worth around twenty million, give or take a million either way. But their seemingly idyllic life hadn't been without tragedy. Their only child, a boy called Cameron, had gone missing twenty years ago in the strangest of circumstances. He had simply vanished off the face of the earth, never to be seen or heard from again.

As I had had dealings with them over the past five years I had got to know them fairly well. When Mrs Oxton told me about the disappearance of her son she burst into tears. Fifteen years later it still hurt her badly and brought on a sadness that was deeply engraved into her consciousness.

Apparently, Cameron Oxton had left the family home in Windsor, where they were living at the time, in the early hours of one morning taking some clothes and his passport with him. He walked out of the front door and disappeared into thin air. Nobody had ever heard from him again. Not even a postcard or a telephone call to his mother. When Mrs Oxton had first revealed the story to me I didn't know what to make of it or what to say. What do you say in such tragic circumstances? Of course, I expressed my sadness and regret. Any consultant trying to impress them would have done the same. After all, the fees I earned from them paid for my wife's beauty treatments. Today, Cameron Oxton would have been forty-years-of-age.

On one of my visits to their home, Mrs Oxton had shown me a photograph of Cameron, taken a couple of months before he went missing. It was at some black-tie bash in town. He had a pretty, classy looking blonde on his arm. He didn't look a great deal like his dad, but more like his mother. Long dark hair and an attempt of a moustache across his top lip. Long faced, gaunt features. On one occasion when I had arrived at the house to see Mr Oxton he wasn't there. He had been delayed by a round of golf that had overrun. Mrs

Oxton invited me into the house, something old man Oxton didn't like when he wasn't there.

On this occasion she had turned very mournful when she told me it was her one and only wish to be reunited with her son. She had even turned to asking a psychic for help, but her husband had forbidden her from employing anyone like that, never mind have such a person in the house.

Not knowing what had happened to him had left a huge gap in her life. She longed to hear his voice and to see his sparking eyes once gain. It had taken her more than a decade to get over his loss, but it was something she would never get over.

For the first time in my life I knew what loss meant, made doubly distressing by not knowing what had happened. I wouldn't wish such a thing on my worst enemy. It got me thinking about my own boys. How would I cope if one of them went missing? I cringed at the thought. At least I had two children. Cameron Oxton was an only child.

On the occasions I had met Mr Oxton to discuss his investment portfolio he had never discussed his son. The subject was off limits. He appeared to be blasé about it, but maybe he was putting on a brave face for my benefit. I put it down to a granite like - whatever will be will be - attitude. He was never -whatever will be will be - when it came to money. He was as sharp as a tack. He wouldn't take second best. He was tight with money. The only expression of gratitude I ever received from him was a second-rate bottle of whisky as a Christmas gift. I found him boorish and a bit of a bully. He had rebuked his wife in front of me on one occasion when she had attended a meeting I had with him in my office. I didn't like him, but I admired him. He was a self-made millionaire who hadn't been born with a silver spoon in his mouth. Far from it.

When Mrs Oxton had shown me the family photograph album I was struck with how Cameron Oxton resembled my one and only brother. They had the same features, the same appealing smile, the same eyes, the same shape of mouth. From the photograph they looked a similar height, weight and build. They were the same age. That got me thinking.

Fifteen years ago, Kevin, my older brother had gone to Thailand to live the life of a beach-bum on the idyllic island of Phuket. He had given-up on the rat-race to lay on a beach and make a living busking or whatever. I understand that after a couple of years he opened a beachside bar and made money pimping local girls to western tourists. The Thai police had threatened to deport him on several occasions but he simply greased a few palms and they left him alone until the next time. I hadn't seen Kevin for close to six years.

After the evening meal, on the day I had been informed I would be dead in a year, I logged onto my PC and found Kevin's email address. First, I constructed a brief message on a scrap of paper, rewrote it a couple of times, changed some of the words then once satisfied I typed it into an email and sent it.

Despite not hearing from him for a while, I assumed he still had the same email account. In the message I refrained from telling him about my condition. He might have been upset. The content of the email was to tell him that I had a proposition to put to him. If the truth be told I didn't know if he would get back to me.

The last time I had seen him, face-to-face, was at our parent's funeral. They had died on the same day when the ship they were cruising on in the South China Sea capsized when it was caught in a sudden massive typhoon which flipped the vessel over. They were two of the hundred people who lost their lives in the accident.

Chapter 3

The following day, whilst I was in my office at work, at a time during the mid-afternoon the telephone rang. Low and behold it was Kevin calling me from Thailand. He asked me what the proposition was all about. He didn't ask how Claire was, or how his nephews were doing. The first thing he asked me was what did I mean by a proposition. I cut it short, telling him that the line wasn't secure; therefore, if he gave me a telephone number I would contact him from home this evening. After a brief silence, he agreed and gave me a telephone number. He said he would await my call then promptly hung up.

After my conversation with Kevin I punched the name, Cameron Oxton, into my file search engine in order to re-familiarise myself with the data I had gathered on his disappearance. There was quite a lot of material. Needless to say, in my role as an investment advisor, I had already done plenty of homework into the strange disappearance of a twenty-year old man from the Windsor area.

The local police had been altered at ten o'clock on a summer evening twenty years ago when Cameron failed to return home after leaving the house that morning. The police were baffled by his disappearance. He had never done anything like that before. The police questioned his parents, the neighbours and his friends to try and build a pattern of his movements. They found nothing. There wasn't a note. Some of his clothes had gone. It was thought that he had taken the small amount of cash he had in the house. There was no obvious motive to why he had gone. The police questioned the Oxton's and asked if there had been a family argument or if any kind of animosity had developed. There was a widespread belief that old man Oxton disapproved of his son's new girlfriend and some of the crowd they hung-out with in the clubs of Soho.

After his disappearance the trail went as cold as post-Christmas turkey. With his passport gone the police came to the conclusion that he had left the country, or that he had been abducted by person's unknown or even aliens. An appeal for information posted by Windsor police drew little response. Someone said they had seen him in Soho the day after his disappearance but this was quickly dismissed as a case of mistaken identity. It was akin to the disappearance of Lord Lucan. Another theory supported by the police was that he had gone to the continent, after all the girl he had been seeing was studying at the Sorbonne in Paris. Maybe he had intended to travel to Paris. Maybe he had fallen off a Dover-Calais ferry, maybe he had been abducted by little green men. At the end of the day nobody knew what had happened to Cameron.

That evening, at midnight, I went into my study and rang the number Kevin had given me. It was six o'clock in the morning in Thailand. To my surprise he answered the telephone straight away. He must have been having a good night along Phuket's club row because he sounded hoarse. I had a secret admiration for my brother because he had found his place in life. As a youth he had always liked to party. Unlike me he avoided any kind of discipline or education. He said he could make money busking in the clubs of Phuket. Then, a couple of years later, he had opened a beach side bar. It sounded as if he was doing okay for himself.

He asked me what the proposition was about. I told him I had an idea of a way that we could make some big money. My next question confused him. I asked him if he could recall hearing about the disappearance of a young man called Cameron Oxton, twenty years ago. He told me to get a life. Of course, he couldn't remember that far back.

I filled him in and told him all about the disappearance. He said so what? People go missing all the time and no he couldn't recall anyone with that name. Why should he? Exactly, I thought. He asked me why I was interested in this Cameron fellow.

I gave him a brief summary of the background. When I mentioned that the Oxton family were rich beyond the reach of most people he seemed to have an idea where this was going.

The tone in his voice suggested that he was surprised that his squeaky-clean brother would ever contemplate anything like this. I asked him if his hair was grey yet. He laughed and said that the sun had bleached it that colour a long time ago. His pale skin was the shade of light walnut veneer. He said he looked like Bradley Cooper with a tan. It was now my turn to laugh out loud.

When I told him that he reminded me of Cameron Oxton he stopped laughing and asked me where I was going with this for a second time. I replied that I didn't know. He suggested that he Skype me. I said too dangerous, but perhaps he could send me a recent photograph of himself because I wanted to see how he looked. He said okay.

In order to keep things secure, I asked him not to telephone me at my place of employment but to email me at home. We didn't want to leave a trail. If this was going to work then we had to be disciplined. He asked if what was going to work. When I told him he was going to become Cameron Oxton to inherit the Oxton millions, he laughed. He asked me if I was serious? I told him I was deadly serious.

The following morning, without telling Claire where I was going, I paid a visit to see Doctor Khan. We chatted for a while about my illness and the symptoms. I told him I was feeling fine, though a little tired. Things were okay at work, though the firm had lost a major client, which had put a strain on things.

Yesterday, I had checked the Oxton investment portfolio. The yield was good. The plan was out performing many others. It had risen by zero-point-eight of a percent in the last quarter, which in times of low confidence on the financial market was excellent.

Khan said he wanted to take another blood sample to see if there was any change in my condition. I said okay. He took another quantity of blood from my arm.

Chapter 4

During my sofa chats with Mrs Oxton I had retained a great deal of what she had told me about Cameron. Everything from his first birthday, to where he went to school, to their first family holidays and so forth. As a trained consultant it was my job to retain information about my clients. I kept two files, one for the firm and one for me, which I kept locked in a bureau in my home. I knew things about them and Cameron that very few people would know. I had also carried out countless hours of desk research, discovering all I could about the Oxton's, Cameron and the case. I knew everything there was to know from the names of the police officers who had carried out the investigation twenty years ago to the size of Cameron's feet, to his favourite football team.

Twenty years was a long time. People change in that time, not only in looks and appearance but in other ways as well. Some in ways they would never have imagined. I hoped that a combination of these factors would result in my brother passing himself off as Cameron Oxton, if only for a short period of time. In that time, I thought that it could be possible that the Oxton's would give my brother money and that he would pass some of it to me.

That night I went to bed and spent an hour looking up at the ceiling, wondering if we could pull this off. Later, that morning, in the early hours, I woke up sweating. I felt a pain in my side. A pain I had never felt before. I wondered if the illness was about to make itself manifest on my body. When I awoke at seven I felt fine.

That day I copied the file I had on Cameron Oxton and sent it to my brother by air-mail. I advised him to study it and become familiar with the facts. Like the name of the dogs the family had and the name of the nanny who had cared for him when his parents were away. The name of the house in Windsor and the names of near relatives such as grandparents and the like. My hours of research had paid off for I knew a great deal about the Oxton family. I counted that some of the things which were not known to me could be put down to a lapse of memory over time. The question was could Kevin impersonate Cameron Oxton?

Would he be able to convince Mrs Oxton that he was her long-lost son returning home after twenty years? There was only one way to find out. That was to try. If they saw through him, they saw through him. By the time they realised that Kevin wasn't their son it may be too late. They could have parted with a large amount of money. The proof of the pudding was trying to pass himself off.

After a lapse of a week Kevin go back in contact with me by email to my home account. He told me he had received the file in the post. He said the scheme was 'pie in the sky', bonkers, but it might work. After all, the Oxton's might be relieved to see their son walk in the door after twenty years in the wilderness they might welcome him back with open arms. The person walking through the door would know things nobody else knew so he had to be their son returning from the dead.

    Kevin said he would study the file. If he thought it could be done he would get himself on a flight home, then we could plan the next steps.

    After a further few days in which I hadn't heard from my brother I was beginning to think that he had concluded that it couldn't be done. Therefore, he wouldn't be coming home. Then I received an email from him which said: 'Coming home to attend the party. Make sure you keep a place for me on the top table.'

    I concluded that meant he was prepared to give it a go. He was booked onto a BA flight leaving Bangkok in the morning on Friday. He would be arriving into Heathrow around six pm UK time. He asked me to pick him up from terminal five. He must have been taking it seriously to travel back home. I was enthused about what we could achieve.

    My next task was to create a backstory to cover the twenty years gap. I knew from the police investigation that Cameron hadn't made it to Paris, because there was no record of him going through passport control in Dover or at the other side of the channel. After considering the facts I came up with the story that he had gone to Ireland on the spur of the moment. Once in Dublin he had met a girl and fallen in love with her. They had then travelled to Bali in Indonesia to join a hippy commune. They never returned. I wasn't convinced myself by this story. It had more holes in it than a leaky bucket but it was the best I could think of. Loads of Brits do go out to the Far East and some never come back, so it was possible. If it was to succeed Kevin had to make it sound so plausible that few would doubt his words. In order to make it more feasible I carried out some research on Bali and created a backstory that read like something from the pen of a skilled writer of fiction.

It took me the best part of a day to put the whole thing together. How Cameron had gone out there to stay for a week, but soon found himself renouncing western values to find Buddhism and align himself to that way of life. Then how he had got a job in a club and how he had been persuaded by a girl to stay for the long term. Twenty years length of long term. It did read like a script from a far-fetched movie.

I was in Heathrow on that Friday evening for Kevin's arrival. Although I hadn't clapped eyes on him for six years, I recognised him the second he stepped through the exit from immigration and into the arrival hall. He was just as tall as he had always been, a lot older and greyer around the edge of his thick hair that had been bleached strawberry blond by the eastern sun. He was still relatively slim and looked in good health. The goatee beard on his chin gave him the look of some wannabe philosopher with great insight into the working of the human mind. I liked his look. It was sort of east meets west.

He was wearing a thin cheesecloth shirt, cut-off jeans and open toed sandals on his feet. He had a kit bag on his shoulder. Knowing Kevin that would be all his luggage.

On meeting we shook hands but didn't indulge in a lot of conversation. He said he was tired and needed some sleep to get over the ten-hour flight and the jet-lag he would face in the coming day.

We left the airport in my car. I took him to the Earls Court area where I had rented a flat for two weeks. My brother was cool. His tanned appearance gave him a slight swarthy Latin appearance rather than a Brit. He came across in some ways as an old hippy who had never grown out of peace, love and understanding.

Once he was settled in the flat I went home. I had called my wife, Claire, at midday to tell her that I would be home late this evening as I had arranged an appointment with a client. I did wonder if she suspected me of playing away but I was hardly a stud, those days had long gone.

The following day, Saturday, I met my brother in a wine bar on Holland Park Road at noon. We chatted in hushed conversation over a bottle of Sauvignon. He told me about his life in Phuket. We reminisced about our childhood. Kevin was only two years older than me so we had been close as kids. Always larking around together and getting into all kinds of scrapes.

The wine bar was quiet at this time of the day. Taped violin music was playing over a couple of speakers. A guy at the bar was slicing lemons.

We shared a bottle of wine and got into deep conversation. We reminisced about our dear parents. It got a bit mournful if the truth be told. He gave me a brief summary of his life as a bar proprietor come beach-bum on the island of Phuket. It was somewhat bizarre that I was an urban everyday Joe who worked in an office in the City of London and he was a mature hippy who had become a bar owner in a beautiful setting on the other side of the globe.

He asked why I had come up with the idea. I pursed my lips and gave a sort of half-hearted shrug of the shoulders.

"Well," I began. "It would be a way of making some money." He didn't ask me if I needed money. "I mean," I said. "Twenty years have passed. The return of the prodigal son might just work."

He agreed. I went on to say that both the Oxton's were getting on in years and whilst there was no evidence of ill health they couldn't live forever. Someone would have to inherit their fortune. As far as I was aware they had no extended family to whom the money could be given. Rather than give their fortune to some underserving charity, Battersea Dogs Home or Her Majesty's Government, why not give it to the returning son?

Kevin gave me a whimsical expression. He said there was no guarantee the returning son would receive a penny. After all, I didn't know why he had gone. I said true, but at least we would find out if that was the case. The Oxton's might fall for it.

Kevin screwed his face into a frown. I knew that look. It was his big brother look. He said he disagreed with my assessment and proceeded to give me his opinion. The returning son would have to pass a series of tests. He would be questioned by not only the Oxton's but the police and even possibly the Missing Person Bureau and what not. Any investigator worth his or her salt would soon uncover the plot. Anyone with half-a-brain would assume it was too good to be true. The Oxton's solicitor would probably look into the background of the man who advised them on their investments. Me. There was a chance they would discover that the new Cameron was in fact the brother of the man who advised them on financial matters.

On reflection, I could see where Kevin was coming from. He had a good point. Background checks of the people who were close to Mr and Mrs Oxton would reveal a connection. It was at this stage that I assumed the plan was dead in the water. I expected him to say something on the lines of: *Good try. Better luck next time*. But he didn't. The next thing he said was to the contrary. He said he couldn't do it for the reasons he had stated, but he knew someone who could.

"Who?" I asked.

Kevin said he knew an English guy in Phuket who had the knowhow and the skill to do it. He named him as Aiden Sheppey.

The name meant absolutely nothing to me. Kev told me that Shep - as he was known - was a former confidence trickster who had left the UK some time ago to start afresh in Thailand, fleecing rich western tourists in a Bangkok property scam. I had to admit that I didn't want anyone else to get involved. Such was my opposition to the idea I was about to say no when Kevin informed me that he had already spoken to Shep. To say I wasn't best pleased by his intervention was an understatement. Once again, my brother had taken it upon himself to lead.

I told him in no uncertain manner that I was annoyed by his intervention. Kevin told me to stay calm. He repeated that it was too dangerous for him to get involved. This Aiden Sheppey had looked over the file I had sent him.

Sheppey was of the opinion that he could do it. Such was his interest that he was coming to London in the next couple of days and would meet up with Kevin and me. Kevin could see that I wasn't pleased about the arrangement but there was nothing I could do. He repeated that Shep was a professional conman who knew how to manage such a situation in a confident and brash manner. He was a clean skin who had no connection to the Oxton's what-so-ever. I relented. I said okay. Whilst I wasn't exactly jumping for joy that someone else was involved I was willing to meet him. That night I went home feeling betrayed to a degree, tired and a little annoyed.

Chapter 5

The following morning, Saturday, Claire and I took the boys to a local supermarket to buy the groceries and what-not for the week ahead. After some lunch in the afternoon, the boys and I went to watch a game of cricket at a local club. It was in the bar during the lunch break that I suddenly felt ill. I was overcome by a dizzy spell, lost my balance and fell to the floor. My youngest son, Ben, started to cry. Several people came to attend to me. One of them was an off-duty paramedic who was there in a part-time capacity. The chap said that I may have an ear infection and if I applied some ointment it would clear up in no time, but it was best to see my GP. I said I would. The damage had been done, my sons had seen me fall. They would tell their mother. She would ask me that the problem was. I would have to repeat that it was nothing. Just a brief dizzy spell.

Sure, enough when he got home Jack told his mum that I had lost my balance and keeled over. Claire asked me what had happened. I told her I had simply had a brief episode of dizziness and fell over. It was nothing. She wasn't convinced.

After that I felt okay for the remainder of the day. I knew that Claire knew that something wasn't right. I had lost my appetite and I hadn't been performing for ages in the bedroom. We had had a healthy sex life, but we had not made love for a while. She didn't want to talk about it but I assumed it would only be a matter of time before she did.

On Sunday afternoon, I had to attend a pre-arranged appointment with one of my clients. This chap lived in South Kensington. He was a wealthy man who had made money from the gambling industry. He liked to pour over spreadsheets of projections and what-not. He would question me for ages on why his investments were not performing as well as some others. I had the stock answer. The market fluctuations were slow to reflect the true value of his plan; therefore, a delay was the reason why. I'm not sure he ever bought it, but after a few glasses of wine and some chat about women he didn't seem to care anymore. To be honest I couldn't really concentrate on him as I was more interested in meeting with this Aiden Sheppey fellow, who according to the text I received from my brother was in the country.

We had arranged to meet that evening at six o'clock in a bar on Fulham Broadway. Aiden Sheppey was staying in the neighbourhood; therefore, it was sensible that we met there.

It turned out to be a pub full of imported beer with Chelsea prices, scores of wooden tables and chairs in a no thrills, bland setting.

Sheppey was a shade under six feet tall, well-tanned, green-eyed, slim, and nicely turned out and reasonably good looking. He spoke in a soft voice and in a kind of elegant manner and had a sophisticated charm that I didn't associate with a conman. But that was his Modus Operandi. He played the role of a high-flying businessman to cheat his way through life. According to my brother he was very successful.

We seated ourselves at a table in the back of the room which was about a quarter full with drinkers. Outside the weather had turned warm. I was conscious of the open setting but I didn't say anything. I felt as if I was being side-lined by my brother who, like always, had taken it upon himself to take the lead. Just like he had done when we were kids.

Sheppey came across to me as a cold-hearted gentleman, just like some of the people I worked with, but he had a cunning, devious streak running through his body. As we downed a pint of overpriced lager we chatted. I have to say that I was impressed with Shep. He told me that before he went to Thailand, he was involved in a number of scams, one which involved impersonating a MP to defraud a gullible millionaire out of some of his money. He didn't go into a lot of detail but as he talked about the story I caught my brother nodding his head in a knowing fashion. He did have form and experience of passing himself off as someone else. At forty-years-of-age he was the same age as Cameron Oxton would be today. Such was his look that I thought he could pass himself off as Cameron Oxton. He was the same height, had the same thin features, green eyes and slim nose. He revealed the plan he had been working on.

Considering what he was planning to do, the plan was brief and to the point. Perhaps this was the way these things were done. I had no idea. Sheppey had studied the content of the file I had sent to my brother. He had memorised everything there was to know, anything he couldn't explain away he said he would put down to a loss of memory. His idea wasn't without merit. I was impressed with the way he presented it. Then it hit me. Here was I someone who hadn't stolen a cent in my life, passing judgement on a conman. What had I become? The question was. Would his plan work?

When I pointed out that Shep was slightly shorter than Cameron. He said so what. Twenty years had passed, he was bound to have lost half an inch in that time. I sort of agreed with him. I have to say that by the time Shep had revealed his plan I had changed my tune. For the first time in a long time I thought there was a good chance we could pull it off. We had a viable plan and a way forward. The enormity of what we were planning to do suddenly weighed heavy on my mind. An attempt to defraud an elderly couple by yanking at their heart strings. Other than that I felt okay.

From here on much of what was going to occur was out of my sphere of influence. To be honest I didn't care. It was perhaps for the best. Shep said he needed a week or so to prepare and to contact one or two people. I didn't like the idea of more people being drawn into the plan, but Shep reduced my fears by saying that this aspect of the plan wouldn't require anyone to know the full scope of the plot.

His idea was for someone to attack him on the street, in full view of onlookers. He would sustain a blow to the head. I nodded my head and said okay as long as my name was never mentioned to anyone outside the three of us. Both Kevin and Shep assured me. Kevin advised me to go home and not to worry. Considering it was me who had come up with the idea in the first place I found that patronising. Was I being marginalised? Possibly, but eh what could I do? That Sunday evening, I returned home to Finchley.

It was another two days before I heard from my brother. He told me that Shep had pulled in a favour and had hired a chap to perform a botched mugging on him. The action was going to take place on a street in Brompton in full view of restaurants. The idea was to stage a fake mugging in which Shep would be hit, fall to the ground and sustain a blow to his head which would result in concussion. It was something he had done previously so he was skilled in making it appear a lot more serious than it was. The diners in a nearby restaurant would witness the attack but be powerless to do anything about it. Kevin advised me to stay away from the Brompton area for the next couple of nights. I ever went anywhere near Brompton.

The thoughts going through my own head considered whether I should end it all, but it was too late. The dye had been cast. It was too late to pull out. There was no other option but to go through with it. A feeling of despair came over me, but there was little I could do. Mixed messages were going through my head. Some said it would be okay. Others that I would die in jail. I tried to relax but I couldn't. I was on edge. The next conversation I had with my brother would be to tell me what had happened; therefore, I couldn't do anything but wait.

Chapter 6

During the following day, Monday, I was able to lose myself preparing a report for a client. It had been one week since I had received the awful news of my impending death. To be honest I hadn't been able to park it at the back of my mind. It was always at the forefront. I felt fine. I had stopped snacking and eating too many sugary things. I had cut down on coffee in favour of bottled water. It made me feel less agitated. I had lost a couple of pounds and had to move the buckle on my belt down one notch. Either I was losing weight because I was eating less or the illness was beginning to attack my body. I had contemplated telling Claire but couldn't bring myself to inform her that I was dying.

It was on Tuesday morning when I received a telephone call from my brother. He informed me that the deed had been done. A report of an incident outside the 'Michelin Star' diner on Brompton Road could be viewed on the 'Evening Standard' web site.

At the time of the call I was just about to go into a meeting with my colleagues in the boardroom, therefore I didn't log on. I waited for the meeting to conclude then I rushed into the office I shared with a couple of colleagues, logged onto my PC and brought up the site. Sure, enough there was a report that last evening a man had been attacked on Brompton Road, in what looked like an attempted mugging of the man's smart phone. A foreign looking man was being sought. The victim had suffered a blow to the head.

He was now in the Royal Free Hospital receiving treatment. No names were given. Just a description of the man the police were trying to trace in connection with the incident. The report was brief but supplied some background detail. The victim, a man in his early forties, had been walking alone when he was attacked from behind. He was knocked to the ground. The attacker had run away in the direction of Brompton cemetery. Several people in a restaurant had witnessed the attack. This wasn't the first case of a mugging in this area. Police assumed the attacks were connected. Though the victim had been hospitalised he wasn't badly hurt.

Once I had read the report, I deleted it from my browsing history. In the next instant my telephone rang. It was Doctor Khan. He sounded exasperated. He asked me to come in to see him as a matter of great urgency. They had received the results of the second blood test.

Despite asking him to tell me the problem he refused to discuss it over the telephone. I left my office at just after one in the afternoon and made it to the practice surgery, which wasn't far from where I lived.

On arrival, I was shown straight into Dr Khan's private office. To be honest I feared the worst. Maybe the first diagnosis had been too kind to me. Maybe I had weeks not months. I was shaking like a leaf when I walked into his office and clapped my eyes on him. He looked as serious as a heart attack. He rarely smiled at the best of times, but his face was bathed in a grim, melancholy expression that said bad news. I feared the worst. I was petrified.

What Khan told me was almost beyond comprehension. Like one of those things you hear about on TV or read in the newspapers but never think it could happen to you. There had been a monumental cock-up at the lab where the blood tests were analysed. Someone - who Khan assumed had been sacked for incompetence - had managed to mix up the samples. My first sample had been mixed-up with someone else. The results from the second sample said there was nothing wrong with me. I wasn't dying from a blood disease, quite the reverse, I was as fit as a fiddle. At worst I was suffering from a mild virus. I mentioned to Khan that I had collapsed in the cricket pavilion. He took a device, looked into my ears and announced that the problem was there. I had an infection in my right ear, which is why I had lost my balance. It was treatable with some wax loosening ointment.

I didn't know whether to laugh or cry. I was livid for a minute then overcome with a sense of joy that I had only ever experienced when my sons were born. Khan was full of remorse and apologies. He said he would understand if I wanted to lodge a formal complaint with the Health Service trust. A number of thoughts circulated through my head. I felt sorry for the poor bastard who had received a clean bill of health, only to be told, sorry that's wrong. I didn't know what to do. I wanted to punch him and kiss him at the same time. I sat in a chair and ran my hands over my face and let out a huge sigh.

Khan looked embarrassed and pained. He said he understood my reaction. Who wouldn't? He asked me if I had told my wife of my supposed condition. I said, no. He let out a sigh of his own. He asked me again if I wanted to report the matter to the NHS complaints panel. If I did he would give me the details of who to contact. The truth is that I liked Doctor Khan. Maybe the next time we played golf he would let me win. I looked at him and shook my head.

"No need" I said. It wasn't his fault that some idiot in a lab had put the wrong name on the blood samples. After a brief period of silence, I repeated that I wouldn't be lodging a complaint and didn't want to take it any further. I had no desire to get anyone into any kind of trouble. I wanted to forget about the whole episode.

Dr Khan had been good to me and Claire when our son, Ben, had bronchitis as a young child. I hadn't forgotten his kindness. He thanked me, apologised again and said that a full investigation to determine what had occurred would ensure it would never happen again. I shrugged my shoulders and told him to move on. At least I wouldn't be dying anytime soon. I asked him if I could use his telephone. He said of course and left me in the office alone to make a couple of calls. First, I contacted a colleague at my place of work and told him I would be working from home for the remainder of the day, then I called home and spoke to Claire. I said I wanted to take her out this evening for a bite to eat at the restaurant where I had taken her on our first evening out after we moved to our home in Finchley. She said okay. She would ask our neighbour to babysit the boys. She asked me if I felt okay. I replied; "never better."

When Khan came back into the room he handed me a prescription for an eardrops solution to clear up the infection in my inner ear. I thanked him. I actually thanked him instead of punching his lights out.

That evening Claire and I enjoyed a lovely meal in a restaurant close to our home. It brought back so many happy memories. Claire looked lovely, she wore the little black dress I had bought her at Christmas and the pearl necklace that was my late mothers.

I had found that our relationship was going through a sticky patch. We chatted as you do and reconnected. It seemed as if we didn't get much quality time these days what with work and looking after two growing boys. I had always hoped we would have a boy and a girl to have the perfect family, but it wasn't to be. The boys were not bad in anyway, but it would have been nice to have had a girl as the second child. I was in a good mood, after all, I had escaped from a death sentence. During the meal I suggested that we get away in the summer and go over to the States to visit some friends who lived thirty miles outside of San Diego. I had long ago wanted to do the Pacific Coast Highway in a little red Corvette. Now that I was going to live I would do it. No ifs and no buts. I was going to do it. Then the reality dawned on me. I was still involved in the plot to swindle the Oxton's. It dampened my spirit a touch. Nevertheless, I succeeded in putting it to the back of my mind for a few hours.

That night, Claire and I made love for the first time in ages. I felt that our marriage was going to get back on track.

Chapter 7

The following morning, I logged onto my home PC and the reality came back to bite me on the backside. My brother had left an email asking me to contact him so he could 'update' me. I somehow hoped he would tell me that Sheppey had disappeared up his own backside. In truth, I was no longer interested in pursuing this stupid get rich quick scheme. Too late.

Kevin told me that Sheppey's plan was working out fine. On admittance to the Royal Free Hospital he had been checked over. When the ward administrator asked him for his name he said he didn't know it. Although there was evidence of a blow to the head the doctors were baffled. Could it be that the blow had caused amnesia? His memory bank had been wiped and whilst it wasn't common it wouldn't be the first or the last time such a thing had happened. As he had no identification on him at the time of the attack there was no telling who he was. Shep had been placed into a ward in order that they could keep him under observation. The police hadn't been called at this time. That's were there could be a problem so it was imperative that this didn't happen because his face could be plastered everywhere. If his condition didn't improve in the next twenty-four to forty-eight hours the hospital authorities would be forced to seek police assistance to determine who he is.

During that day, I stewed things over in my mind. Claire had been in touch with our friends in San Diego. They were happy for us to come over to visit them and to bring the boys. Claire said she would check the flights and perhaps we could spend a couple of days in New York City on a stopover. The boys would love the Big Apple. The shock of being told that I was dying from an incurable disease, then to be told I wasn't, had given me a fresh perspective on life. For the first time in a long time I wasn't worried about the materialist things in life. I concluded that - touch wood - I did earn enough money to make things meet and to ensure that my children had a decent future. The materialistic things like a new car every year, expensive holidays, home entertainment centres and what not didn't mean a damn thing. I concluded that when you have been to the brink and looked over the edge they didn't mean much. Then I asked myself who was I kidding? Then the Oxton's and the attempt to commit a crime came back to me. At one point I was considering contacting Kevin to tell him I wanted to pull out. It wouldn't be as easy as that. The get rich quick scheme had been my idea. If I went to prison my life would be as good as over. If I contacted the Oxton's and requested an appointment to see them I could explain everything and hope they would take pity on me, forgive me and not get the police involved. Who was I kidding? Oxton would report me to my firm, the police would become involved and I would be in court quicker than you could say, 'Jack Robinson'. I would do a year, maybe two. My brother would do the same. He would dislike me even more than he did now. Sheppey would get some of his mates to give me a good beating. Claire would divorce me. The boys would turn their back or me. What had I done? I was effectively in a cul-de-sac with no way to turn back.

After twenty-four hours in an observation ward Shep was transferred to a recuperation ward. He told the nurses he was having flashbacks and his memory was imperceptibly beginning to reboot. He said he thought his name was Cameron and that he had once lived in the Windsor area as he recalled playing in the great park as a kid and sailing on the River Thames in his father's motorboat. The hospital staff quizzed him in an attempt to draw out more information. That evening Shep told a consultant that he thought his name was Cameron Oxton. The dye was cast. That was all the hospital needed to get on the case. The hospital contacted the Missing Person Bureau. The bureau said they would search their database and get back in touch with the hospital. Meanwhile the hospital searched the NHS database for a Cameron Oxton. Sure, enough there was a Cameron Oxton registered as living at an address in Windsor. The record went blank twenty years ago. Several hours later the Missing Person Bureau got back in contact with the hospital to tell them that a Cameron Oxton was on the list of missing persons, having been reported missing twenty years ago.

The hospital staff asked him if he knew his date of birth. He was one day out. They asked him if he knew his parents' names. Sheppey said his father's name began with a D. Donald or Daniel or something like that. Then he recalled it was Derek. How about your mother's name asked a nurse? Sheppey said he thought it was

Gillian or Gwen. It was enough, Genevieve, was her name. The hospital got back in touch with the bureau. The person with the mild contusion on his head could be someone who had gone missing twenty years ago.

This was now going to be a police matter. The following day a police inspector from the local station paid Sheppey a visit in hospital. He asked him where he had been for the last twenty years. He replied he didn't know. Everything was a blank. He couldn't remember anything of his past from the second he woke up on the pavement after hitting his head.

That evening the same police officer and a woman colleague visited Mr and Mrs Oxton at their home in north London. He told them to brace themselves for an incredible shock. There was a possibility, all be it a possibility, that their son, Cameron had been located. Mrs Oxton was overcome with emotion, to the extent that the family doctor had to be called to give her a sedative. Derek Oxton was literally stunned into silence. The woman officer asked Mr Oxton for any photographs of Cameron, or if he knew of any distinguishing marks Cameron had. He said that Cameron had a birth mark on his right knee in the form of a blemish about the size of a finger nail. Needless to say, this was something Mrs Oxton had told me in passing. I had written this information into the file I had produced. Little doubt that Sheppey had somehow made a blemish mark on his right knee. Though it could have faded over time. The police asked the Oxton's if young Cameron had any pets as a child.

Derek Oxton said that Cameron had been given a rabbit by his late uncle Cyril, called Bouncer for his seventh birthday and later a ginger cat called Carrot.

That evening the police officers went back to the Royal Free to interview Sheppey. They asked to see his right knee and sure enough there was a trace of a small blemish on the knee cap. The guy asked Sheppey – Cameron – if he could recall the name of the rabbit he had as a pet. Sheppey replied Bouncer. When asked who had given him the pet he replied it was his Uncle Cyril. What clinched the deal was that he knew the cat was called Carrot. The officers went straight back to the Oxton's and informed them that it looked highly likely that the man in a ward in the Royal Free was their missing son. He had risen from the dead. Mrs Oxton, who was still under sedation, was informed of developments by her husband. She cried. Mr Oxton could only shake his head and ask the officers where his son had been for the last twenty years. The lead officer said he had no idea because Cameron had no idea. It was a mystery beyond words.

Despite being under orders from the family doctor not to overstress herself Mrs Oxton said she wanted to see her son at the first available opportunity. The police had no problem with that. They took Mr and Mrs Oxton to see the man in the hospital ward.
The reunion of a son, seemingly lost and gone forever, took place at a time around ten o'clock that evening. The parents were

accompanied by their doctor who was also a close friend. He had treated Cameron so he would be able to identify him as well. When Mrs Oxton was helped into the room and clapped her eyes on Sheppey she nearly collapsed to the floor. He was exactly how she imagined he would look today. Mr Oxton looked on not knowing what to make of it. When the police asked the doctor if he could recognise him he said he was ninety percent sure it was Cameron.

The Oxton's family doctor asked to speak to the consultant neurologist on duty. He was taken to meet her by one of the nurses. Oxton's doctor asked her what could have happened in this case. Simple she said. Cases like this, though not common, were not unheard of. Twenty years ago, there was a possibility that Cameron had been involved in some kind of traumatic event that erased his memory. It was common in some cases of mental illness and drug taking. There was no suggestion that Cameron had ever taken any kind of drug. More than likely it was a case of an accident which caused a blow to the head. The consequence of this was that his memory had been affected and that he thought he was someone else. The blow to the head he had sustained the other evening had reversed the effect. His short-term memory had been erased to allow his long-term memory to come back so he was able to remember things from his childhood. It was a one in a million occurrence but not beyond the realms of possibility.

Mrs Oxton did not want to leave her son's side. Shep laid it on thick doting on his mother calling her Ginny, a pet family name. He could see that everything he had been told about the Oxton's was true. They were moneyed, though old man Oxton was down to earth and the kind of guy who called a spade-a-spade, whereas Mrs Oxton was the one who could be easily duped into believing that her baby, her forty-year-old son had returned from the dead.

I didn't want to speculate on what was going on in that hospital room. When I thought of the criminal deception taking place I felt sick. In a way I hoped if not expected a knock at the front door at any time and for the police to arrest me. The knock didn't come.

A day later Sheppey or Cameron Oxton as he was now known was transferred into the private Cromwell Hospital in west London to recuperate at a cost of four thousand pounds a day. The Oxton's were urged to prepare for their son coming home in the next few days. The police and the hospital had put a news blackout on the case. Not one word of this was to be leaked to the media. The interest from the media would have been enormous and would only result in news correspondences camping outside of their house for days on end. They would soon regret the day he ever came back.

Chapter 8

I returned to work the following day. My diary was full of appointments. In a moment of down-time I looked at the British Medical Institution web-site and read the complaints procedure, but I quickly put it out of my mind. I had given Khan my word that I wouldn't pursue a complaint against him or the practice, therefore I couldn't go down that route. I was pleased that he had the balls to tell me and that I hadn't told Claire. She would have gone ballistic and gone straight to the newspapers. Thankfully, I had kept quiet. She had booked us onto a flight to New York, a one night stay in Manhattan then a flight onto San Diego the following day. I was looking forward to seeing our friends and showing the boys around southern California.

The next day I was in the office for ten o'clock. My diary secretary, a delightful young lady called Melanie, advised me that I had received a telephone call from Mr Derek Oxton who had requested that he come in to see me on a highly confidential matter.

I hadn't seen that coming. I was put on edge. I asked myself if I should inform my brother that Oxton wanted to see me but I decided against it. Kevin wouldn't have an idea why Oxton wanted to see me. I asked Melanie to contact Mr Oxton to tell him I would be able to meet him at any time, after all he was one of my priority clients. Low and behold she told me that Oxton wanted to see me that afternoon in my office at two o'clock. I had no alternative but to say fine.

My office was on the south side of the Gherkin building in central London on the tenth floor so I had fantastic views across the city and across the river to the spread of south London in the distance. On my desk were framed photographs of Claire with the boys, taken at various times and locations over the past couple of years, along with papers and the usual desk furniture. As the time crept towards two o'clock I felt my trepidation increasing. Why did he want to see me? Did he have an inkling that I was behind the sudden reappearance of his son? I contemplated my response to such an accusation, then I wondered why I was getting so uptight. If I kept my cool and didn't stutter I would be okay. I wasn't cut out for this pressure. But this wasn't pressure. Being told I would be dead in a year was pressure. I had come through that. Everything Mrs Oxton had told me about Cameron had been done when her husband wasn't in attendance, consequently unless she had told him he would have no knowledge that our chats had ever taken place. I tried to put it to the back of my mind. I would be obliging and thoroughly professional in our dealings.

Oxton arrived at a shade before two. He was on his own. This was the first time he had been in my office since the first time I had met him five years ago. He was wearing a grey business suit, shirt and silk tie. He looked every inch a man with affluent tastes, but streetwise at the same time. And he didn't go in for anything too ostentatious like an expense watch or fancy jewellery. He still had a blunt north of England accent and an attitude. Melanie showed him into my office. I noticed that he never looked at her legs, unlike me. I smiled and held out my hand. We exchanged a firm handshake. Despite the fact that he was in his early seventies he still had a firm grip.

Rather than have the meeting in the office, I took him down the corridor and into a private meeting room. I invited him to take a seat by a low desk. I joined him at the other side. I placed his investment file on the desk between us. The file contained all his investment details, spreadsheets, projections, yields and the like. I asked him if he wanted a drink. A coffee or something stronger. He said no thanks. He said he didn't have a lot of time as he was meeting some people later in the afternoon. This would only be a brief meeting. Melanie, my assistant, left the room and closed the door behind her.

"What can I do for you?" I asked.

Oxton looked at me through his heavy grey eyes. He waited for a few moments then said. "I've got a situation."

I remained expressionless, though I was aware of a lump in my throat. I could only say. "Nothing serious. I trust."

"Someone who says he's my son has appeared on the scene."

I wriggled in my seat, then crossed my legs. I could only say "oh". I was thinking that I had to remember that he was my client, not my victim.

"What can I do for you?" I asked.

He didn't reply straight away. He glanced out of the window and took in the view of the river and the sleek steel and glass rapier of the Shard building rising into the clear sky.

He looked at me. "I don't think it's him," he said. I didn't know if he was telling me this or if it was a question. "In fact, I know it's not him." I didn't say anything but wondered how he knew this. He was talking in contradiction. "I want you to set up a fund for my son. Transfer three million from my account in an account for Cameron Oxton," he requested.

I felt the content of my stomach shift. I didn't say anything for a few seconds before I said. "I can do that for you. If that's what you wish."

We looked at each for a few seconds. I didn't want to say anything that would lead to him asking me questions. It was his money he could with it as he pleased.

"That will make her happy," he said.

"Her?" I asked.

"My wife. She's convinced it's our son. But I'm going to hire a private detective to investigate this further."

I nodded my head. "Have you informed the police of your suspicion?" I asked.

He sucked in air through his teeth. "They're convinced he's genuine," he said in a scornful way. I didn't want to question him further. I assumed that his next appointment was with a private detective agency. I got back to the task in hand.

"I can set up an account in the name of...." I stopped myself from saying Aiden Sheppey right at the last moment. I said... "Cameron Oxton."

"In his full name. Cameron Leech Oxton," he said.

I knew that Leech was his mother's maiden name. "How quickly do you want me to do this?" I asked.

"As soon as possible. Then write to me to say that it's been done, then I can show the letter to her and my..." he paused to run his hand over his mouth. "son." He said in a disparaging way.

"As you wish," I said.

With that Oxton got up out of the chair. I didn't want to carry on our conversation and by the way he was stepping to the door, neither did he. It was obvious to see from this exchange that he had seen through the charade, but he was willing to go along with it for the time being or until such a time when the private investigator he was going to employ uncovered the plot. At least he didn't accuse me of being a conspirator. I showed him to the door leading onto the corridor and on to the elevator. We parted with a handshake.

I returned to my office and closed the door. I wondered what to do next. The alternatives were to do nothing or to inform my brother that he was going to employ a private detective. Oxton obviously suspected foul play. Why he hadn't informed the police of his suspicion was a different matter, but maybe he had. Maybe there was a lot more to this than met the eye.

After a few moments to think it over I contacted my brother on his mobile phone. I told him of my meeting with Oxton and what he had said to me.

Kevin said Oxton was bound to be suspicious but in reality, there was nothing to stop Sheppey from being his son and if he couldn't prove it he didn't have a leg to stand on. I thought his words were a bit odd in the extreme. As if he was convinced that Sheppey really was Oxton's long lost son.

Kevin asked me to keep him updated should I hear from Oxton in the next couple of days. I said okay. When the paperwork to set up the account in the name of Cameron Oxton was ready I would let him know. It would be done by the end of the day. Kevin said 'good'. I didn't know if he had something up his sleeve but I was sure that he and Sheppey would've some kind of a back-up plan. Something they had failed to run by me.

Chapter 9

Working quickly and diligently I soon prepared the paperwork to transfer three million pounds into a new account for Cameron. That afternoon, I asked Melanie to put a recorded, special delivery envelope to Oxton into the post. The letter inside reflected his request to set up an investment account in the name of Cameron Leech Oxton and to transfer three million pounds from his holdings into the new account. The envelope contained a document called a 'Memorandum of Agreement' that had to be signed by both Derek Oxton and his son. Once the letter was received by old man Oxton all he had to do was to contact me and I could make an appointment for me to visit him in order to bring the paperwork to be signed.

That evening, Kevin sent me an email. Shep was to be discharged from the Cromwell Hospital tomorrow. He would be residing with the Oxton's to recuperate and get to know his parents all over again.

Once the money was in Cameron's account he would be entitled to do whatever he wished with it.

I felt that things were coming to a head. We would either be found out or it would actually work. It could be all over in a few days come-what-may. Sheppey could transfer the entire value of the plan into another account. He would then be able to transfer some money to my brother for his cut and a cheque for me for my share. The money would be gone and nothing could be done about it.

Simple. The following day he could walk out of the Oxton's house and never be seen again. What could go wrong? Plenty. For a start Oxton had his doubts. Something told me he might just go along with it then blame his wife when the man disappeared for a second time with three million pounds of his money. I felt awful about it. It was a stressful time for me.

When I arrived in the office the following morning I asked my assistant, Melanie, to check if the recorded delivery letter had reached the Oxton's. She checked the reference on-line and informed me that it had been signed for at the address. Now it was just a case of waiting for Mr Oxton to get in contact with me. In the hours since we had met I wondered if he had employed the services of a private investigator. I was still pretty dumfounded at my brother's reaction. He didn't seem to be that worried, so maybe I shouldn't have been.

I would be going to the Oxton's with a fistful of documents. Sheppey or Cameron would have to be there to sign the investment agreement; therefore, it would be me, Oxton and Sheppey. Mrs Oxton need not be there if she didn't want to be.

It was mid-afternoon when Melanie came into my office to inform me that Mister Oxton had received my letter. The startling aspect was that Oxton wanted to conclude the signing straight away. Melanie said she wasn't aware that the Oxton's had a son. I said something on the lines of, yes, they have a son who's been out of the country for the past twenty years.

She looked at me in amazement and shrugged her shoulders. I thought that her shrug just about summed up things pretty succinctly. I considered it prudent of myself to make the appointment with Mister Oxton. I didn't want him to think I was hiding from him so I contacted him by telephone. He asked me to be at his home the following day at one o'clock in the afternoon. He was collecting his son from the Cromwell Hospital this evening.

His son would be at the house tomorrow to sign the papers. I said okay. I laid it on thick and told him I was looking forward to meeting his son. He didn't reply and ended the call. I thought our conversation had gone well in the circumstance.

At the conclusion of the call I contacted my brother on his mobile. We chatted for a couple of minutes. I told him the end game was nearly upon us. It was nearing the time when Sheppey would inherit three million pounds. It would be his to do whatever he liked.

When I ended the call with my brother I got up from my seat, went to the window and looked across the flat spread of the city to the south. A tour boat on the Thames was edging under Tower Bridge. It was a glorious day, dominated by a dazzling sky the shade of turquoise. Since I had been told I might not make it into old age I had seen the beautiful things around me in an almost afterglow like wonder.

Once home, I had a couple of beers and played touch-rugby with the boys in the back garden. After they had gone to bed, Claire and I talked in the conservatory. It was the first time we had had a good chat in a while. She informed me that she wanted to find a part-time job and get back to work doing something. There was a job in a local estate agent for a part-time agent. She had worked in an agency before so it wasn't something she didn't have experience of. I advised her to go for it. I thought that she had something on her mind. I asked her what it was. She said she wanted to leave London and return up north. I had to admit that I didn't see that one coming, but it made a lot of sense. London was becoming far too overcrowded, and the crime, and the pollution were not good for our children. The schools in the area were not that great. She said if we went to live in the Harrogate area the boys would have a better quality of life. I wasn't sure if that was the case, but I didn't disagree with her. I said we should think about it and start looking at property in and around Harrogate to see what we could buy if we sold this place at the current market price. I only hoped that I would be able to go with her because if Sheppey was uncovered as a fraud the whole house of cards could come crashing down around my ears.

That night I didn't get a lot of sleep. I tossed and turned my way into the small hours, then I got up early, made some breakfast at six-thirty and went into work early. Once in the office I checked my diary for the day, looked through the morning paper for ten minutes then I prepared the papers for the meeting with the Oxton's. I placed the 'Memorandum of Agreement', the transfer document and the investment papers into my briefcase. My email was empty. I had remembered to delete all emails from both my home and work account and empty the recycle box. I had deleted the file containing all my research on the Oxton family. I was fairly sure that I had covered my tracks as best as I could. The morning went slow. I did some work on a couple of other clients.

It was twelve o'clock when I informed colleagues that I was going to visit Mr. Oxton on business. I had my briefcase with me containing all the essential documents, which I had checked at least a dozen times.

I didn't want to use public transport because of the sensitive nature of the documents in my possession, so I flagged down a Hackney cab and asked the driver to take me to Bishops Lane in Highgate. It was a nice day. The first warm day of spring. I loved London at this time of the year, the noise, the smells and the pace of life. The colour and the diversity. It was truly a wonderful cosmopolitan city, but after my talk with Claire last night it was perhaps time to move on and seek a better quality of life elsewhere.

It took the cab a little over twenty minutes to drive the couple of miles into Highgate.

Chapter 10

The Oxton's resided in a large five bedroomed property along a secluded road. It was a huge red brick house, sandwiched on a road that ran between Hampstead golf course to the west and Highgate golf course to the east. It must have been worth between three to four million pounds at today's prices.

Derek Oxton's old style Mercedes was parked on the brick courtyard behind a walled partition. I stepped through the central gate and approached the front door which was under a porch veranda. I noticed the CCTV camera at the door aimed at me. I had a tight hold of my briefcase. Before pressing the doorbell, I checked that my tie was straight, then I pressed the doorbell. I ran a hand over my brow to wipe away a smattering of sweat. It was warm. I was perspiring and I did feel nervous as I didn't know what awaited me inside.

The front door was opened by a middle-aged woman I had never seen before. She was wearing a matching blouse and skirt. I assumed she was a maid of some description. She didn't smile. I introduced myself and told her Mr Oxton was expecting me. She showed me into the large hallway reception with a chequered tile floor and double stairway leading to the first floor. She led me across the floor to the wide double door that led into a sitting room. I had been in this house on several occasions therefore I was familiar with the layout. Oxton and I usually conducted business in his study, but it looked as if we were going to do the signing in the sitting room.

The maid opened the door and showed me into the room. Derek Oxton and the man I knew as Aiden Sheppey were sitting around a flowery sofa in the centre of the room aside a long low table that was strung with newspapers, magazines and some papers. I noticed the large photograph album. Maybe Mr Oxton had been showing his son the family photos. Maybe he had come to the conclusion that he really was his flesh and blood.

I glanced around the room noticing the fine furniture, the items of artwork and the expensive crystal object d'art. It was a room with a female touch. To the right where a set of French windows that led onto a patio that in turn led to steps going down to a lawn that was almost as long as the fairways of the golf course the property backed onto. The doors were partially open so a faint breeze was coming in.

As I entered Oxton looked at me and the briefcase in my hand. The maid closed the door behind her to leave the three of us alone. But no sooner had the door closed then my attention went to the French doors as they opened and a man I had never seen before entered the room. He was a tall, distinguished looking man in his mid-to-late-sixties in a nicely cut suit and neatly styled grey hair. Oxton looked at him but didn't introduce him to me. I was put on edge by the sudden appearance of this stranger. He was a big guy with large arms and a massive chest. Maybe he was the private investigator Oxton had hired. If he wasn't, then who the hell was he? I assumed he had uncovered the plot and was about to deliver the damming evidence. I don't mind telling you that I felt an ache in my stomach.

I quickly glanced at Sheppey but he had his head down looking at something on the table. It was as if he was averting his eyes from me on purpose.

Oxton shifted his posture in the chair he was sitting in.

'I'd like you to meet my friend and family doctor Sir Alan Bartok," he said. The chap stepped across the floor, around the table and stood next to the chair Oxton was sitting in. I ran my tongue across my lips to wet them.

"Nice to meet you," I said.

Sir Alan didn't reply and just gave me a frown.

"Have you brought the paperwork?" Oxton asked and gestured for me to join them at the sofa. I had stalled as soon as Bartok had appeared on the scene.

"Are you coming to join us?" Oxton asked me.

"Certainly," I replied.

"Sit next to my son."

I moved across the floor to the sofa. I wended around a chair and sat on the settee at the other end from Sheppey. I could feel the palms of my hands around the handle of the briefcase were leaking. I felt a large bead of sweat roll down my forehead. I placed the briefcase on the table top, unclipped the two latches and opened it wide to reveal the documents inside. I extracted them and put them down on the table surface.

Oxton coughed. "Okay. Let's cut the crap here. I know this man isn't my son."

I looked at him in slack jawed amazement. The blank expression on the face of the man standing beside him didn't change. Aiden Sheppey didn't move a muscle or say a word.

"How do I know?" Oxton asked.

I had no idea if he was asking me a direct question or if it was a statement. I moved my eyes to Sheppey, who leaned back into the comfort of the backrest and crossed his legs. I detected that he knew something I didn't.

"I'll tell you. Shall I?" said Oxton. I looked at him with a confused, aimless, gormless look on my face. "Because Sir Alan and I buried him twenty years ago. That's how I know."

I gulped on none existent moisture in my throat. "My son died of a drugs overdose giving to him by his *girlfriend*. We had to bury him in an unmarked grave."

It was as if I had suddenly lost the ability to understand the English language. It was akin to a scene from some weird dream sequence. Maybe it was a nightmare. I had to pinch myself to know this was no dream or nightmare. I blew out a deep breath.

"But I'm pleased he's come back. I've not seen my wife happier than the day you came back." I was astounded. "Therefore, even though I know the truth of this. I'm prepared to go along with it." I was even more astounded by what he had said. "We...." Oxton looked at Sheppey… "have had a good, man-to-man chat and we've come to an agreement. Isn't that right Cameron?"

Sheppey replied with a resounding. "Yes."

"For three million pounds he has promised that he'll be my son. That way my wife's broken heart will be mended."

Sheppey nodded his head. I quickly summarised that Oxton had known all along that this was an attempt to steal money from him. But he didn't care. A surrogate son had appeared to fill the gap left by the death of Cameron. It was a bizarre situation. Almost too strange for adequate words.

"Pass me those papers," Oxton requested, gesturing to the documents I had brought with me.

I did as he requested. I handed him the papers. The man next to him, this Dr Bartok, took a step towards him to witness the signing. Oxton scanned his eyes over the 'Memorandum of Agreement', then flicked through the pages of the investment agreement and the transferred deed.

"This looks to be in order," he said.

Dr Bartok slipped a hand into a pocket and extracted a gold body writing pen which he handed to his friend. Oxton placed the papers on the table and duly signed the memorandum and the transfer deed with a quick swipe of his right hand. Then he passed the papers to his son and asked him to counter sign the memorandum and the transfer document, then sign the agreement.

Oxton watched him sign the papers, then he sat back into the seat.

"I know what's gone on here and so do you. I've never told anyone this before. It stays within these four walls. Agreed?" He wasn't aiming his words at one individual but all of us. Dr Bartok, Sheppey and I responding by saying a unified 'yes'.

"This way you get the money and my wife gets a son back. Knowing what really happened to Cameron would have killed her, exposing you would only kill her again so this is a win-win. Agreed?"

Sheppey nodded his head. "Agreed," he said.

The business had been done in the most bizarre of circumstances. Oxton never directly accused me of being involved in a scam, though I assumed he may have had his suspicion. As he said it was a 'win-win'. His wife. The woman who had given birth to his son had him back in her life and Sheppey had access to three million pounds. All he needed to do was to keep his end of the deal. If he didn't Oxton had the resources to come gunning for him. He knew people!

Once all the papers had been signed I collected them and gave both Oxton and Sheppey copies. I placed the third set into my briefcase. It was only a few minutes later that I left the house for the final time.

To be honest I didn't care if I never received a penny of the money. I wasn't dying of an incurable disease. I didn't need a huge amount of money to live on. I had something far more precious. I had life.

When stepping out of the house I looked up at the blue sky and breathed in a deep breath. At least I had made an old woman very happy. She would live to the end of her days in the knowledge that her son was alive. I thought that profound.

Chapter 11

Ironically; perhaps, four weeks later. The firm I worked for informed me that another larger investment bank was buying them out. The firm would be downsizing and all the jobs were in jeopardy. I knew I wasn't high enough in the pecking order to be saved. This news actually came as a great relief to me because the job was becoming mundane. I needed a new challenge.

Two months later, I was made redundant. I was just another investment broker on the 'rock and roll'. In order to relief the stress of losing my job the firm gave me a decent leaving present. I was offered a package of two year's salary, plus fifty thousand pounds in back bonuses. I was given a cheque for nearly three hundred and fifty thousand pounds. I was given a company car free of charge for six months and enrolled onto an executive job search.

Losing my job came as a timely heads-up to my wife who vowed to reduce her spending habits. She didn't.

Three months after I left the firm we put our house on the market for two and a half million pounds. It sold the next day for the full asking price. We moved up north to the Harrogate area, close to where Claire was born. The boys were still young and not settled in their schools in London, so it wasn't such a big upheaval for them. I enrolled at a local college to do a Certificate in Education. I got a job with a local private education provider teaching Accountancy.

I never did see any of the money Aiden Sheppey inherited. I suppose he may have given some to my brother or maybe he just liked being Cameron Oxton, so he didn't care about the money. Maybe he spent his days playing golf with his old man. Maybe Oxton had taken to him so much he made him his heir to his fortune. I did exchange a couple of emails with my brother who had gone back to Thailand. I never knew if he got some money. I was glad I was out of it. At least I never had to meet Oxton again or shake hands with his prodigal son. I was happy on that score.

I did get to California. I hired a little red Corvette and drove my wife and sons along the Pacific Coast highway with the roof up.

I often reminisce about this episode in my life and reflect on the craziness of it. If it wasn't for some fool getting the results of my blood test confused with someone else, I would never have gone through with it. Then Mrs Oxton would never have been reunited with her missing son. I put it down to fate, but it certainly taught me a lesson that money wasn't everything in life. There are more important things to consider. Like health, well-being and family ties.

The End

The Stalker

CHAPTER 1

Someone, he couldn't recall who, had once told Newman that you're nobody if you don't have a stalker. Being stalked by some obsessive fan is about the highest accolade a star could have. That got Newman thinking. Why didn't his client Liam McAndrew have a stalker? Liam was a very successful TV soap star. Someone who was in the public eye. Was it that he wasn't appreciated enough? Surely not. He had been voted as the sexist guy in a British soap last year by the readers of a women's magazine for the second year running. He came second in a 'rear of the year' poll. What the public didn't know about Liam McAndrew was that he was gay. It was well-known in soap-land but he had yet to come out of the closet as far as the public was concerned. It wouldn't do his stud, man about town, lady killer character any good what-so-ever. Therefore, his real life sexual orientation was hushed up. Liam McAndrew played Ryan Steadman in the BBC day-time soap, 'Connaught Place'. Steadman played the part of a devious, back stabbing bastard who had attempted to bed most of the female characters in the soap. In it, he was the owner of a wine bar called the, 'Winery', which was one of the most frequently used sets.

People in the public spotlight who were less well-known than Liam McAndrew had a stalker. A stalker could boost an actor's image and value to the producers and the marketing people with tales of how they had been followed by a fan who just couldn't get enough of them.

If Liam had a stalker it wouldn't only boost his ego but make him box-office and persuade the soap producers that he was worth keeping on, because if the rumours were true some of the bosses in big boss house were looking to bin him when his contract came up for renewal in six months. They said that he had been in the show too long, that the public wanted to see new faces and have new blood that would signal a change in the storylines, re-invigorate the audience and draw in a younger demographic.

Peter Newman, agent to a stable of soap stars thought that Liam McAndrew needed to reclaim his mojo; or else his commission and Liam's income would take a bit of a nosedive if he was written out of the soap.

The problem was that you can't simply go into a store or go on-line and order a stalker. Stalkers don't advertise their services in the small ad columns. Stalkers are special people. Though they can be extremely dangerous people. An example being, Mark Chapman, the murderer of John Lennon, and the case of John Hinckley who attempted to assassinate US President Ronald Reagan in order to bring himself to the attention of actress Jodie Foster. That is when stalking and obsession go very bad and into another league. In the main, the vast majority of stalkers are just misguided harmless people.

Newman undertook some desk research on stalking. He had to think of a way of getting one of his cash-cows back onto the gossip pages of the tabloid newspapers. He would do anything to prevent Liam McAndrew falling out of favour with the bosses in soap-land. Whilst achieving this through publicity about a stalker was an option, it wasn't by any means the only one.

Peter Newman had not only been an agent to the stars for thirty years but also a publicist who knew how to generate publicity for his flock.

The Newman Agency, worked out of a small office in a building close to Euston Road, just around the corner from the entrance to Euston railway station. He was an agent with a reputation as someone who fought hard for his clients. Having been in the game for more years than he cared to remember, he was the daddy of all agents. At nearly seventy-years-of-age he had seen the influence of TV soaps on the culture of the nation and the increasing number of productions from the outset of the dawn of the square box.

His office was just a two-room affair. Glass framed photographs of his clients lined the four walls. A signed photograph of a couple of A-listers was placed on his desk next to the telephone. His Personal Assistant worked from an office across a communal corridor. A couple of arm chairs were set in front of his desk. A matching sofa along one side. The usual backdrop.

Newman had been thinking about Liam McAndrew for a while. How was he going to raise his star with the producers and get him back into the gossip columns? He had an idea. He was going to team-up McAndrew with an actress from a rival soap. Her name was Tess Delaney. Get them seen together around town and get the tongues wagging. Was Liam McAndrew dating Tess Delaney? She was the voluptuous blonde from a rival ITV soap, 'Electric Avenue'. The thrice weekly daytime soap much loved by lonely housewives, the retired and the work shy. Were they an item? Was it a TV love affair? As they were photographed canoodling in front of the paps long lens cameras, viewers would be asking those questions.

Liam McAndrew was on route to his home in west London after recording, 'Connaught Place' at the BBC studios in Manchester. He stepped into Newman's office. Simone, Newman's PA showed him into her boss's office. Joel, Liam McAndrew's boyfriend was lurking in the background. Liam told everyone that Joel was his minder. At six feet tall, fit and with a lean body Liam hardly needed a minder. He was a very handsome guy. Dusky skinned, dark wavy hair. Slender nose and thin lips, capped white teeth and a chiselled granite chin. Deep, dark bedroom eyes. If the eyes make the man than he was the Casanova portrayed in the soap backstory.

Newman greeted Liam with a firm handshake and an agent's backslap. Joel parked himself on the settee beside Newman's desk. Newman eyed him, smiled, but didn't say a word. He concentrated on Liam who was dressed in a dark, modern cut, pin striped jacket with matching pants and a waistcoat over an open neck light blue shirt. The diamond stud in his ear lobe sparkled.

Liam sat in front of the desk. Newman was sitting in the seat that backed onto a window with a view across the square in front of the railway station. He opened a file that Simone had placed on his desk. It contained the history of Liam's career and contract with the producers of, 'Connaught Place'.

"Let's talk shop," said Newman. "We know from rumours that the producers are looking to let several of the cast go," he muttered.

Some huge hiatus at Christmas would see several of the cast killed in a minibus crash as they travelled to a Christmas party. A drunk driver would be blamed; therefore, enhancing the 'don't drink and drive' message at Christmas.

"I assume I'm one of those in the frame," Liam said in a three-quarter whisper.

"Word has it that you'll go," Newman replied candidly.

"Kinell. I've been on there for eight years for God sake. Now they want me out," said Liam.

"It doesn't mean to say it's all signed, sealed and delivered," said Newman trying to comfort him.

"My contract ends in six months. Is there any talk of a new one?"

"Not at the moment."

"Have you asked?"

"I've asked. They're non-committal at the moment."

"In that case they're writing me out. My scene time is being reduced week on week."

Liam turned to look at his boyfriend. Joel was listening to the conversation.

"We have to get you back on the entertainment pages," said Newman.

"What more appearances, opening stores?" Liam asked in a sarcastic tone.

"Not exactly."

"I don't know if I can be bothered anymore."

Newman leaned forward and set his elbows on the desk. "I've got a few ideas. One is to start dating Tess Delaney. Be seen around town with her. Get some tongues wagging. We'll get some agencies to run the photos and copy them to the tabloids."

"Have you spoken to her?" Liam asked.

"She's keen on the idea," said Newman in a positive manner.

"What else?"

"A few appearances on TV. The new series of, 'Through the Keyhole'. We can get you on there. 'Loose Women'. Celebrity quiz show appearance. Things like celebrity 'The Chase', 'Pointless.' We'll get on the One Show. Paul O'Grady. Room 101. All the chat shows."

Liam crossed his legs. His tasselled louvers shone with the same veracity as the diamond stud in his ear. He threw his head back, glanced at his wristwatch, then at his lover and they exchanged a blank expression. There was nothing he could say. If he wanted to get back in the newspapers and have his name back in the headlines he had to do what Newman suggested. Newman had gone off the idea of the stalker. The idea was a little too left field, even for him.

CHAPTER 2

Liam reluctantly dated Tess Delaney. She played a character called, April Banks in 'Electric Avenue'. In it she played a hard-nosed, hard drinking businesswoman who ran her own model agency with a strict rule book. In real life she wasn't much different from her character. It was like art imitating real life. Or was it real life imitating art? One or the other. She was a peroxide blonde with big assets and an even bigger personality. Cast members on the set of, 'Electric Avenue', called her 'Petulant Polly'. She was known to be a bit of a diva and difficult to work with.

Newman had contacted a couple of London photo agencies to tip them off, so a couple of paps turned up with their Nikon cameras and zoom lens to capture the moment they entered a West-End restaurant whispering sweet nothings and holding hands. It was all an act. They knew it. The paps knew it but the public fell for it. At the end of the night they would leave in a taxi which would take them to Delaney's flat in South Kensington. Liam would stay for an hour then once the way was clear he would take a taxi to his home in Kew. In reality the Delaney and McAndrew relationship was purely platonic.

The plan worked. A couple of photographs made it into the gossip columns of the fifty pence tabloids, under the heading: 'Are Ryan Steadman and April Banks an item?' Then some rubbish about how they shared a cheeky kiss in a top West-End restaurant whilst eating pizza. With the tag line, 'Ryan gets a *pizza* April.'

Newman's master plan was up and running. Next, he managed to book them onto the Christmas edition of, 'Celebrity Who Wants to be a Millionaire'. Filming took place over a weekend at the end of July. He hoped that by the time of the broadcast both of their stars would have risen, allowing them to negotiate lucrative new contracts with their respective soap masters.

Liam had to be in Manchester for two days of the week to shoot episodes of, 'Connaught Place', then he would fly to Heathrow to hook up with Joel Braviro in the cottage they shared in west London. Joel was a Brazilian national who had lived in the UK for the past ten years. He met Liam McAndrew, two years ago, at a party given by a friend of a friend and they had been partners ever since. Meanwhile, Liam was obliged to see Tess Delaney at least twice a week. If there was a photo opportunity to be had, then it had to be taken. He had accompanied her to the Annual Soap awards, then the Annual TV awards. He would even go to Crufts to be photographed with her stroking an ugly Pitbull if it achieved the objective. There were several aims but only one objective. To keep them both on their respective soaps.

The added publicity seemed to be working. Throughout the month of June, Liam had appeared on a couple of late-night talk shows and even got a mention on BBC One's nightly prime time,

'The One Show'. The bargain-bin celebrity magazines had featured him on a couple of occasions over the past month.

Newman was working his old magic. His experience of the publicity game had manipulated the perfect scenario. McAndrew and Delaney both experienced an upturn in their celebrity status. Liam's writers were increasing his camera time. He had more lines. His story lines increased along with his presence on camera. She also reaped the benefits, with various extra non-soap appointments. Such as a guest spot on, 'Loose Women' and an invitation to participate in some charity promotion. It all contributed to greater exposure in the cut-throat world of daytime TV soaps. Which in some respects were real life soaps? Such was the back-biting and bickering amongst the cast behind the cameras.

Liam McAndrew's fan-club secretary contacted him to say his fan-mail had increased by twenty percent since he had been in the papers. The number of requests for signed photographs had doubled. The number of people who wanted to hire him for promotional work had gone from zero in May, June and July to five offers in August.

It was when Liam was in the studio filming an episode of, 'Connaught Place', that he was asked by the producer, a man called Roger Hampson, to pop into the office as he needed to speak to him about a delicate matter. Liam had no idea what the delicate matter was. He had not broken any of the company's golden rules. He had been on time, all the time. He hadn't done anything to upset his employees. His contract did allow him to do extra promotion work.

It was with a certain amount of trepidation that he went to the meeting in the TV company's headquarters. Present were Hampson, Head of Cooperate Affairs, Shelia Devaney, and Head of Personnel, Jill Lambourne. All three were sitting in an office with a view over Salford Quays to the new office and apartment developments that had transformed this part of Manchester docks from an eyesore into one of the UK's most vibrate and modern settings.

Liam entered the meeting room on the fifth floor of the building. He greeted those gathered there. Roger Hampson had a file in his hand. Both Devaney and Lambourne didn't have any papers in front of them.

Hampson greeted Liam and asked him to take a seat. Hampson was at the best of times a serious man. Liam couldn't recall a time when he had seen him smile or crack a joke. He wasn't smiling today and he wasn't telling any jokes. He was only in his early thirties. He was the new kid on the block. New to the soap production line but good at what he did. He had been brought in by the production company to bring new ideas and a new direction. He had a reputation as someone who wasn't afraid to swing the axe.

Liam made himself comfortable. "What can I do for you good people?" he asked.

Hampson loosened the knot of his tie. It was something he did without knowing why.

"Liam, we want you to know that we've received a couple of letters from someone who seems to be how can I say, for want of a better word *bonkers*. Someone has written to us saying that he's going to kill you."

Liam swallowed hard. Jill Lambourne, an attractive woman in her mid-forties with neat dark hair and a trim figure, a TV career professional, shifted her posture in the wrap around seat.

Hampson continued. "It's not the first time we've received correspondence like this from fans, but these are particularly nasty. It talks about beheading and all sorts of gruesome things."

"We thought we'd better make you aware of them," said Lambourne.

"There's probably nothing in them but you need to be aware," he added.

Sheila Devaney looked to Liam. "The letters say that if you keep meeting with Tess Delaney then he will murder you. We know that's all about your profile and we understand that. That's not the issue. The issue is that we need to protect you until they stop. We haven't yet, at this stage, informed the police. But if they continue we'll inform the necessary authorities. With your agreement of course."

"The letters are here. Would you like to see them?" Hampson enquired.

Liam wasn't sure if he did or didn't want to read them but thought what the hell. If someone was threatening to kill him then he might as well read them if not only to satisfy his own curiosity but to see what the nut-job was saying.

"Yeah. I'll have a look at them," he said.

Hampson got up from his seat and stepped around the table. He placed a plain manila type paper wallet into Liam's outstretched hand.

He opened the file and withdrew the contents. There were four A4 sized white sheets containing typed text. Attached to them were several photographs taken from a morning tabloid newspaper and others from a TV gossip magazine. The photographs showed him and Tess Delaney arm-in-arm as they left one of the West-End restaurants they had used for a photo opportunity. There was also a glossy photograph of him, one his fan-club would have issued. Missing a vital part of his anatomy, namely his head.

He read the content of a letter dated one week ago. It was a rambling tirade of abuse and threats. Basically, the writer wanted him to end it with Tess Delaney or else he would have to take serious action against him. He said he had a machete and he wouldn't hesitate to use it to attack him and decapitate him.

Liam felt a tremble. They were clearly written by someone who had a screw loose. What he did notice was that the language and the quality of the constructed sentences were not written by someone who had a good grasp of written English. The writer didn't have a decent command of words, vocabulary and ability to write in English. There were a number of common errors. They were either written by someone who was semi-illiterate or by someone who didn't read English that well.

"This is one angry person," Liam said.

"That's why we decided to share them with you," said Hampson. "It's probably a crank, but better to be safe than sorry. We suggest you keep your guard up and be aware of who is around you."

Liam thanked Hampson. "Have you spoken to Tess Delaney's people about these?" he asked.

"Not yet," he replied.

"Perhaps you may wish to inform your agent," Shelia Devaney advised.

"Okay. I'll do that," said Liam. He was at a loss at what to do. He had heard of this kind of thing before but it had never happened to anyone he knew. He wondered how to tackle it. "Do you have any advice?" he asked.

"I know it's easy for me to say it but try not to worry too much. It's probably a prank, but at the same time use common sense and don't be alone," Hampson said.

Liam considered them wise words, but scary ones at the same time.

"Do you want us to go to the police?" Sheila Devaney asked.

Liam looked at her and blew out a sigh. "To be honest I don't know. Maybe not at this time," he said.

"We respect that decision," she said.

"Can I keep them?" asked Liam.

"What we'll do is give you a set of copies," said Hampson. He used a phone to summon one of the administrative staff, a girl called Amanda, to come in to take a copy of the letters and to give one set to Liam.

Amanda came into the office. She took the documents from Hampson. When she came back a few minutes later she gave the originals back to Hampson and handed a white A4 envelope, containing copies to Liam.

CHAPTER 3

Liam was at a loss what to do. After some thought he decided his agent should know so he put in a call to Peter Newman at his office in London. He told him of the meeting and the topic of the discussion he had just had. Newman asked him to fax the letters to him or better still ask one of the staff to scan them then email them directly to him. Liam asked Hampson if he would do this for him. Hampson said of course. He would ask Amanda if she would see to it immediately.

Newman contacted Liam within the hour of receiving the email with the attachment. He told him not to worry; the writer of the letters was obviously a crank. Some idiot who got off threatening celebrities. He reminded Liam that he and Tess Delaney were contracted to be guests on a late-night talk show the day after tomorrow in London. It would air the following night. He advised him to go ahead and appear as planned. Liam said okay. He asked Newman if Tess Delaney had ever mentioned anything about a stalker or some nutcase writing to her. Newman said she had never mentioned anything like that to him.

McAndrew and Delaney appeared on the pilot of a talk show, 'Tonight with Alan Mellon', that recorded at the BBC's White City studio. The host was a one-time stand-up comedian, Alan Mellon, who had gone from telling jokes to interviewing a lot of C-list celebrities and basically taking the Michael out of them, but in a nice way. Liam didn't mind. It was screen time. After the interview Tess and he had to play a game of identifying other soap stars from multiple combined faces. It wasn't Rocket Science. It was standard easy watching TV fare. Nobody, especially the viewers didn't have to work hard. The programme was due to air at eleven-thirty the following evening. Liam then went up to Manchester to record two episodes of, 'Connaught Place'.

On the morning following the screening of, 'Tonight with Alan Mellon', Peter Newman contacted Liam to tell him that he had seen the show and that he and Tess had come across really well and had got into the spirit of the show. Alan Mellon just happened to be another one of Newman's clients.

CHAPTER 4

Liam got a feeling that something wasn't right whilst he was sitting at a gate in Terminal A in Manchester Airport. He was waiting to board the nine-thirty morning shuttle to Heathrow. He had taken a fleeting glance at a TV screen. Sky News was on. He saw a headline flash on the screen. Something about a prominent theatre and TV agent had been murdered at his home in London last night. The volume was low so he couldn't hear what was being said above the gaggle of sound from the activity around him.

The item went off to be replaced by an advertisement. Without knowing why, he had a feeling that it involved Peter Newman. Something told him. Maybe it was the cold shudder he had just felt or the beads of perspiration that had suddenly surfaced on his brow.

He took out his cell-phone and put in a call to Newman's Euston office. There was no response the first time so he tried again two minutes later. This time the call was answered on the third ring by a male voice that was unfamiliar to him.

"Yes," the person asked.

"Is Peter Newman there?" Liam asked.

"Who is this?" the person enquired.

"It's Liam McAndrew. I'd like to speak to Peter. Or his PA."

The voice didn't reply immediately. There appeared to be a moment of reflection.

"How do you know Mr Newman?" asked the person.

"He's my agent. I'm Liam McAndrew. I play Ryan Steadman in Connaught Place."

Silence for five seconds before another voice came on the line. "Who is this please?"

"Liam McAndrew."

Liam could hear the chap saying, 'Liam McAndrew' as if he was telling another person who had a list of names on a sheet. "What is your connection to Peter Newman?"

"He's my agent."

He could hear a sharp intake of breath.

"I'm sorry to inform you that Peter Newman was murdered last night in his home. My name is Detective Inspector Paul Berryman of the Metropolitan Police."

Liam was stunned beyond words. He could only repeat the word *murdered*, under his breath.

"Where are you calling from?" The man who called himself DI Berryman asked. Liam didn't reply immediately. "Sir. Where are you calling from?" he asked again.

"Manchester Airport. I'm waiting to board a plane to Heathrow."

"On your return to London would you please call me on this number." He read out an eleven-digit number. "We are seeking to interview all his clients." He repeated the number, purposely pausing after each digit so Liam was able to enter it into his phone.

"What happened?" he asked.

"We are still conducting initial enquiries at this stage. We shall have a clearer picture later today." He replied with a detective's patter.

"Who did it?"

"We don't have a suspect in custody at this time. I would appreciate it if you would contact me on your return or speak to one of my colleagues. Will you do that?"

"Yes. No problem."

"Thank you. Mr McAndrew. We'll meet shortly. I wish you a pleasant flight."

"Yeah. Thanks."

"Thank you."

The call ended at that point.

Liam looked at the happy smiling faces of the people around him. People on vacation. People with laughter on their faces. He wanted to cry but was too stunned to do that. He had known Peter Newman for ten years. Now he was gone. His life taken by an unknown murderer.

After a few minutes he was invited to board the aircraft. He wondered for a few brief moments if he wanted to take the flight, as if it was all connected to the murder of Newman. That someone was on board who wished him bad. He quickly discounted that and boarded with the rest of the passengers.

Once in Heathrow, Liam put in a call to a fellow actor and friend, called Tom Snowdon. Snowdon told him what he knew about the murder of Peter Newman from the news that had aired on the TV channels. The latest was that Newman was murdered on the front step of his own home. Apparently, he had left this office at eight o'clock last night and had taken a tube to his home in Highgate. CCTV showed him leaving a tube station and walking alone. He may have been followed. It was believed that someone forced themselves into his house and stabbed him in the doorway. Or the person may have been waiting for him to return. It had shades of the Jill Dando murder, but clearly not such a big profile figure.

Liam's second call was to DI Berryman. He introduced himself and the reason for the call. Berryman thanked him for his call. He took some personal details then suggested that he and a colleague called DC Tyson come around to see him at his home if he agreed to this. Liam said okay. He had nothing to hide and would gladly help the police find the murderer.

CHAPTER 5

Liam lived in a cottage that backed onto River Thames on the south side of the river at Kew Bridge. His front room afforded a view of the parkland at Kew Green. The front elevation was covered with honeysuckle winding his way up a climbing frame to the underside of the bedroom window. He had lived here for the best part of twelve years. Three of them with his Brazilian lover. Their favourite pub, 'The Greyhound' was just a decent stagger away, though he hardly got in their nowadays.

It was seven o'clock in the evening when a car carrying two men in civilian clothes pulled-up in front of his home. Obviously, detectives. They stepped to the front door of the house and rapped on the brass horseshoe knocker.

Liam greeted them at the door. They displayed their ID to him. DI Berryman was a stout guy. Tall with a rounded girth. He had smoked grey, spongy brillo-pad like hair. A thick moustache across his upper lip. He looked to be in his late forties. He had red cheeks and a vein covered nose.

His colleague, DC Andrew Tyson was of mixed race. A younger, clean shaven, good looking man with smooth skin, nice eyes and a cute smile. Shorter than DI Berryman in height and girth.

DI Berryman was wearing a thigh length Burberry type coat over a suit jacket. A striped tie that looked remarkably like an old school tie. Tyson was wearing a short gabardine type raincoat over a plain white shirt, and hipster like pastel trousers.

Liam showed them into a lounge. Joel Braviro was sitting on a two-seater sofa. He got up and stepped into the kitchen as the cops came into the room. The room was small. It had a sofa, a Parker-Knoll type recliner in brown leather with a matching footstool. A small TV was perched on a metal table. Monet prints on the painted walls. A wicker shelf unit contained paperback books, glossy hardbacks and plants in red-orange clay pots.

Berryman made himself comfortable. He sat on the settee then hitched his long legs forward as if the seat wasn't big enough for his backside. DC Tyson remained standing in the doorway. He looked around the room then out and up the stairs to the first-floor landing. Berryman took a notebook from his inside jacket pocket. Liam sat in the recliner and perched his legs on the footstool.

Berryman maintained his down to business face throughout.

"How long did you know Peter Newman?" he asked. The questions were predictable. Did he know anyone who had commented negatively about Newman? Did he know why anyone would want to harm him? Liam said no to both questions. He didn't know why anyone would want to harm Peter. He was the gentlest, most genuine man in the industry.

DC Tyson observed the Q&A session. He never said a word and just continued to look around from his position near the door. Berryman asked Liam about his movements last night, just to dismiss him from their enquiries. Liam said he was in Manchester staying in the flat he rented on Deansgate. He had got there at about seven pm, after spending the entire day recording episodes of, 'Connaught Place'. He had something to eat, watched some TV then read for an hour. Tyson asked him what he was reading. He said he was halfway through a novel by a writer whose name he couldn't remember.

It was at this stage that Liam thought he had better tell them about the poison pen letters he had received. He said he had something to show them, asked them to excuse him for a second, then went upstairs to the bedroom to collect the envelope containing the letters.

He came back down the stairs, into the room and handed the envelope to DI Berryman.

"I received these a week ago. I think you'd better have a look," he advised. Berryman and Tyson shared a face. Berryman opened the envelope and extracted the white sheets and the newspaper printed photographs. Tyson edged forward a couple of feet to peer over his colleague's shoulder.

Berryman read the typed content word for word. "Do you know who sent these?" he asked.

"Not a clue."

"Where are the original envelopes?"

"Roger Hampson will have those."

"Who's Roger Hampson?"

"My producer up in Manchester."

"Can you give me his telephone number?"

Liam gave him the telephone number of the production company HQ in Salford.

"Did you tell Newman about these letters?"

"Yes. I did."

"What did he say?"

"Not much. He said it was probably the work of some nut."

"Who is April Banks?"

"She's in Electric Avenue."

"Is that on television?"

"Yes."

"Is that her character name?"

"Yes. Off screen she's Tess Delaney."

Tyson interjected. "I've seen her in the gossip columns. What's your connection with her?" he asked.

"Our agent paired us together to raise our profile while the producers decide if they're going to give me a new deal."

"A new contract?" Berryman enquired.

"Yes. My deal runs out at the end of the year."

"Is there a chance they won't renew?"

"There's always a chance they won't. That's working in TV."

Berryman's moustache seemed to twitch. He looked at Tyson who remained as cool as a block of ice.

"Who knows about these letters?" Berryman asked.

"Roger Hampson, Jill Lambourne and Sheila Devaney. And the writer."

"Who are Lambourne and Devaney."

"The two women executives in the production company."

"Can I keep these?" asked Berryman referring to the letters.

"Yes. Be my guest. To be honest they giving me the collywobbles."

Berryman didn't say anything.

"Do you think there could be a connection between the murder and those letters?" DC Tyson asked Liam.

"I don't know. Might be a nutcase on the loose."

DI Berryman cleared his throat. "As far as I know from colleagues. Nothing was stolen from Peter Newman. Not even his wallet or his watch so robbery does not appear to be the motive at this stage."

He got up off the settee with a struggle. "We'll leave you in peace. We'll be in touch," he added.

"Are there any developments in finding Newman's killer?" Liam asked.

Berryman said yes. He told Liam that in the next couple of hours the Met police were going to release a CCTV image of a person they believe followed Newman out of the tube station.

"We'll let you know of any developments. In the meantime, if I was you I'd keep your wits about you. If you should see anyone lurking around, looking suspicious let us know." He delved into a jacket pocket and pulled out a business card. "My direct number is

on there. Give me a call if you have to. Thank you for your time."
He handed the card to him.
Liam showed the detectives to the door. They wished him good evening.

At ten-thirty the late evening local BBC London news came on. It featured an item on the Newman murder and the CCTV image Berryman had referred to. It showed a man who may have followed Newman to his home in Highgate. It wasn't anyone Liam knew. He couldn't understand why anyone would follow him, only to kill him on his doorstep when he could have done that in the quarter of a mile or so from the station to his house. It didn't add up.

CHAPTER 6

The murder of Peter Newman reverberated throughout the TV industry. His obituary in 'The Times' was impressive. Everyone had nothing but good things to say about him. The obituary in the trade bible, 'The Stage', was well written.

The funeral took place on a Thursday in the second week of July. One week to the day after the murder. Newman was laid to rest next to his wife who had died five years earlier and their only child who had died at an early age. It was so sad. The congregation was filled by the great and the good. Some of the big wigs at the BBC and ITV turned up. The industry came out in force to pay their last respects. It was a tragedy. A few cast members from Coronation Street, Emmerdale, Hollyoaks and EastEnders were on parade. As where those from, 'Connaught Place', and, 'Electric Avenue'. Some of them were his clients or had been clients in the past. The roll call from Connaught Place was impressive. Jezz Turner who played Lord of the Manor, Sir Peter Williams, Sandra Klein who was Molly Upton and Andrea Janson, a Latvian lady, a newcomer to the cast who played a Polish waitress called Marie in 'the Winery', attended. Stephen Harper who played Leo Castle, Steadman's nemesis in the soap was also there. The press pack from both the print media and television were there in big numbers.

DC Tyson attended the funeral. As the mourners were coming out of the cemetery chapel he took Liam aside and told him of a new development in the hunt for Newman's killer. At ten o'clock this morning someone had come forward to say that he was the person walking behind Newman. He lived in the same area as Newman. He wasn't following him. He was walking home.

Things began to take an increasingly disturbing twist the day following Newman's funeral. Doris Parrish the lady who ran the independent 'Liam McAndrew Fan-club' contacted him to tell him that she had received a very disturbing letter in that morning's post. The writer said Liam McAndrew was a, 'dead man walking'. The letter had been typed on a computer. The content was rambling and contained all sorts of veiled threats. She said she was shaken by the contents and the picture of a headless corpse.

Liam asked her what the postmark said. She went away for a few seconds to check. When she returned she told him that the envelope had been posted in Manchester. He asked her to post the envelope, the letter and the picture straight to DI Berryman by same day, special delivery. He gave her the address on his business card. He then contacted Berryman and told him to expect the letter in the post.

That afternoon Liam asked a local firm to install a security alarm and to fix anti-tamper devices to the windows of his cottage. He was scared. Joel told him that is what the writer wanted. He wasn't wrong.

The following day, Liam flew to Manchester to film two more episodes of the soap.

He was agentless. Has were about four dozen other actors. Whilst it wasn't imperative that he needed anyone to negotiate for him he thought it would be a good idea to get someone on his side, soon.

Has he had been contracted to do it he recorded a Christmas special edition of, 'Celebrity Who Wants to be a Millionaire', with Tess Delaney as his partner.

They got to thirty-two thousand pounds before they were stumped on a question about football. He didn't know anything about football and neither did she so they were well and truly buggered. Alas their 50/50, phone a friend, and ask the audience had gone with the previous three questions. Still they walked off with thirty-two thousand pounds. Half went to his charity choice, the McMillian Cancer Trust; the other half went to her charity, Battersea Dogs Home. He enjoyed doing the show.

After the recording he took Tess to dinner. He asked her if the police had been in touch. She confirmed that they had. They had asked her if anyone had written threatening letters to her, or if she was being stalked. She said she wasn't. Despite her high profile on 'Electric Avenue' playing a character with the charm and elegance of 'Janet the Ripper' she had never received any negative fan attention.

Two days later there was another letter his time to a celebrity obsessed TV magazine gossip columnist by the name of Rod Diamond. Diamond wrote a column in a magazine called, 'The TV Chat Room'.

Diamond contacted the production company, scanned the letter and emailed it to Roger Hampson. The content was much the same as the other two letters. The date in the top left-hand corner. The same structure. Threats, then accusations of all sorts of things Liam was supposed to be doing to Tess Delaney. He wasn't good enough for Tess Delaney. If it wasn't for the threats to murder him, they would have been funny. Still no clue as to who was sending them.

Roger Hampson passed the letters straight onto DC Tyson at New Scotland Yard. The next day Liam was back in London. The security firm had installed an alarm system in his home. They had also fitted anti-tamper locks to the windows. The box on the front, next to the honeysuckle frame, looked out of character with the rest of the façade. So what? It might deter anyone from trying to break in.

CHAPTER 7

It was three in the morning when both Liam and Joel were awoken by the sound of breaking glass. In the quiet of the early morning hours the sound seemed to be far sharper than it would have been in the daylight hours. The sound was replaced in a matter of seconds by the crackle of fire and the orange glow reflecting in the bedroom window. Someone had thrown an explosive device through the front downstairs window.

Panic ensued. They quickly got out of bed. Liam looked out of the window. Flames were licking up the face of the cottage. The sound of glass exploding downstairs was combined with the sound of fire and the smell of smoke. The cottage was on fire.

"Quick, quick get out," shouted Joel over the sound. Liam wanted to keep his modesty. He grabbed his robe and swung it over his shoulders. He was in a state of shock though his survival instincts were kicking in. He went to the bedroom door, opened it and looked down the stairs to the front door and the entrance to the lounge. Smoke was escaping from under the lounge door and moving up the stairs like a slowly gathering grey moorland mist. Thankfully, he had closed the lounge door last night when he came to bed, therefore it was preventing the fire from spreading onto the stairs. The area at the front door was still intact. He looked back into the bedroom where Joel had slipped on his robe.

Liam quickly went down the stairs through the developing mist of smoke. He got to the front door, opened it and stepped outside. Blue and orange flames were gushing out of the downstairs front window like a twisting, swirling out of control world wind. The blue tip was as sharp as a red-hot poker. The flame had leapt up the wall to the underside of the bedroom window which suddenly cracked from top to bottom with the heat. The climbing frame and the honeysuckle had gone.

The next thing he felt was Joel at his back pushing him along the path towards the edge of the road. One of the next-door neighbours, Molly, had come out of her cottage. She was on the path, wearing a lemon dressing gown over pyjamas. Other neighbours further along the row were emerging into the night like zombies coming out of the woods. Someone shouted, are you okay?

Neither Liam or Joel responded. They were too shocked by what was happening to the cottage to speak. The flames coming out of the window were now leaving a black scorch mark on the plaster.

"As anyone called the fire brigade?" someone shouted.

"We have," came a distant response.

"Get away from there," an unknown person advised.

Liam and Joel stepped across the narrow road to the edge of the green. All they could do was observe the cottage going up in flames.

Molly from next door came to join Liam and Joel on the edge of the green. The traffic along Kew Bridge road was nonexistence. No one would have seen or heard the arsonist. It was three o'clock for crying out loud.

The London Fire Brigade were on the scene in less than seven minutes. The sound of their arrival and the general commotion along the road alerted the landlord of, 'The Greyhound', pub which was only a couple of hundred yards away. All the locals could do was watch the incredible sight of the flames shooting out of the downstairs, front window.

The fire brigade sent two engines. They did a brilliant job in getting the fire under control in no time at all and extinguishing the flames. Their quick reaction had saved the cottage from total destruction.

As soon as the fire was under control the lead fireman sought out the owners. He asked them what had happened? Simple, said Liam. Someone had thrown a device through the front window. The lead fireman called the police immediately and asked for a fire investigation team to be summoned.

An hour passed. The firemen were now mopping down and directing water into the front room through the smashed window. A pall of steam was coming out.

It was six o'clock, three hours after the attack, when the fire engines left. Liam and Joel spent the next hour looking at a slowly reducing cloud of steam coming out of the gap where the front window had been. The cottage was a ruin, though the structure was saveable.

At seven in the morning they went into the pub and spent the next two hours in there with the landlord and a couple of the neighbours, being comforted and drinking numerous cups of coffee. They were still numb as to why anyone would wish to burn them alive in their beds. Obviously, the letter writer had taken it up a notch. If it wasn't serious before. It was serious now.

A London Fire Brigade investigation team arrived at ten o'clock. One was a large, hirsute chap in uniform who drove an LFB vehicle. The other was a pretty dark-haired lady who arrived in another car. Liam and Joel met them outside the cottage and looked at the scene. The fellow said his name was Peter Hutchinson.

He was an okay kind of chap. Wide shoulders and a barrel chest. Perhaps forty-five years-of-age at a guess.

The investigation duo stepped across to the LFB vehicle, delved into the boot and extracted several items of equipment. Then they slipped into identical red overalls, before entering the cottage through the front door. It wasn't long before the chap came out, went to the car and opened the boot. Liam asked him if he had found anything. He said they had found a charred house brick. It looked as if the arsonist had attached a bottle full of inflammable liquid to the brick with tape, ignited a cord then threw the brick through the window. There were pieces of shattered glass on the floor and the trace of a flammable liquid. The flames had left a tell-tale residue that suggested the liquid was every-day petrol.

Hutchinson asked Liam to excuse him while he went in and finished his tasks. He had to take some photographs and would finish up. Then he had a report to write which would be forwarded to the police and to Liam so he could pass it to his insurance company. Liam had not even given a thought about that. He thanked Hutchinson for the information then left him to get on with it. Hutchinson went back inside the cottage to join his colleague.

It was thirty minutes before DI Berryman and DC Tyson arrived. They took one look at the front of the cottage and could only shake their heads in disbelieve and rub their hands across their mouths. The letter writing had escalated it to nothing short of attempted murder. The only lead they had was gone. The chap who had come forward had been eliminated one hundred percent from their enquiries.

There wasn't a great deal they could tell Liam. Other than the letter writer had clearly upped his game. It was serious. He and Joel could have been trapped in there and burnt to death. They had been lucky to get out unscathed.

DC Tyson advised Liam to keep a low profile. Did he have anywhere to stay? Liam said he had no shortage of friends he could stay with. That didn't worry him. What worried him was that someone was trying to kill him.

DI Berryman said that until they catch the arsonist then there was little they could do. He did admit that the murder of Peter

Newman and this attempt could be linked. But again, there was no hard evidence. Basically, he didn't know.

As the fire investigation team emerged both Berryman and Tyson went to chat to them. The lady investigator had a set of papers attached to a hardback clipboard. She read her notes to the detectives. No doubt telling them what they had found. The charred brick, the shards of glass that were not consistent with the window glass. The tell-tale residue that pointed to petrol being the accelerant. Attempted murder by arson does not get much more serious.

Liam returned to the pub. He put in a call to Roger Hampson to inform him what had happened. Hampson was stunned. He advised him to come up to Manchester with Joel. The company didn't want the press sniffing around. The production company had a grace and favour flat in Manchester City Centre. He could use it until all this had blown over. Liam thanked him for the offer. He told Hampson he would pack a bag and get up there on train. Joel would be coming with him.

CHAPTER 8

On the train going north, Liam did some thinking. He detected a pattern to this. The letters appeared to come after he had been on TV or in the papers with Tess Delaney. The first one came after they had been featured in the tabloids has secret lovers. The second after they had been on 'Tonight with Alan Mellon'. The third after they had been on 'Celebrity Who Wants to Be a Millionaire'. The difference with 'Who Wants to Be a Millionaire' is that no one knew he was appearing on the show as it wouldn't be aired until Boxing day. That got him thinking. Was it someone who knew his schedule? It narrowed the field down considerably. Who knew his schedule? Who knew he would be at home last night? Who knew that he lived in that cottage? As the train cut through the countryside he began to establish a list. Newman's assistant Simone, unlikely. Someone in the production company, possibly. Tess Delaney, unlikely. He couldn't recall if he had told anyone else that was doing a slot on the quiz show other than a couple of the actors on, 'Connaught Place'. Steve Harper who played Leo Castle for one. Harper wouldn't be behind it. No chance. Maybe it was all purely coincidental. Nevertheless, as the train pulled into Macclesfield station he put in a call to DI Berryman to run the theory by him.

Berryman said his theory was interesting. Then he went on to reveal something far more interesting. He reported that a man, possibly of eastern European appearance had been seen lurking around the southern end of Kew Bridge by a passing police car in the early hours of that morning. This could tie in with the fact that the letter writer didn't have a good command of written English.

Berryman told him the man was carrying a plastic bag. A man of similar description had bought a litre of petrol from a service station just across the bridge in Brentford at around two in the morning. They would have the CCTV from the petrol station in a couple of hours, along with a statement from the person who had served him. The strange thing was that he didn't have a car and had put the petrol into a plastic container, the kind many motorists carry as a reserve. This may be the suspect who had fire-bombed his home. Whilst Berryman asked him to be cautious about expecting an early breakthrough the connections were beginning to come together. It was possible that the suspect had poured the petrol into a glass bottle, then disposed of the container in the river or in a bush somewhere. Berryman said he would keep him posted if he had any further updates. Liam thanked him.

On arrive in Manchester, Liam and Joel took a cab to the production office in Salford Quays. Roger Hampson and Jill Lambourne were there to meet Liam. They chatted for a short time then Lambourne gave him the key to the flat in a block in the centre of the city. Liam and Joel were back in central Manchester within the hour.

CHAPTER 9

The 'grace and favour' flat was in a ten-story apartment block at the back of Piccadilly railway station. The view from the balcony on the seventh floor gave a panoramic view of platform thirteen as the trains came and went and the commuters standing on the platform waiting for their train to arrive. The relatively low-level rooftops of central Manchester were spread out to the Derbyshire peak district in the distance.

Joel had been to a local supermarket to buy provisions for a couple of days. That night they stayed indoors, watched TV and chilled. After the day they had had they just wanted to relax. The shock of what had happened to them that morning at three o'clock would stay with them for a lifetime.

It was at about ten o'clock in the evening when there was a knock at the front door. Liam was in the bathroom. Joel didn't think it was anything suspicious after all who knew they were here. He went to the door and opened it to see who was calling. As soon as the door was open a figure on the corridor lunged at him. Joel caught the glimpse of a metal blade swishing towards him. He instinctively put his hands up to fend off the incoming blow, in doing so he was able to divert the end of the knife from its intended target - the centre of his chest. The tip of the knife entered his chest in the soft, fleshy area below his left shoulder. Joel let out a shriek. But Joel being Joel he wasn't going to take it lying down. He swung a punch at his attacker and managed to crack him on the upper arm. The blow caused the attacker to lose his balance and drop a long dagger to the floor. It hit the floor with a clank of metal on tile. Then Joel felt the pain in his body. Still he kept his eyes on the man, anticipating another attack. The man in front was dressed all in black, sweatshirt and trousers. He was only average height and physique. Fair complexion and colouring. He was wearing a baseball cap on his head pulled down low over his forehead. It was the face of a mature man, perhaps in his mid-to-late thirties.

Now that his weapon was on the floor he chose not to bend down to pick it up in case Joel whacked him. He looked at the knife for the briefest of moments then turned and bolted and ran down the corridor. Joel stepped out and watched him run away at a rate of knots, then through a door that led onto an internal staircase. It was all over in seconds and he was gone. Joel was going to pursue his attacker but when he glanced at his shoulder he could see the blood coming out of his upper chest.

"Liam," he shouted.

Liam emerged out of the bathroom drying his hands on a paper towel. He raised his head to see Joel coming towards him holding his left arm across his chest. Blood on the t-shirt. A grimace on his face, then Liam looked passed him to the open door and the dagger laying on the floor.

He helped Joel into the lounge, then he made a 9-9-9 call. Once he had assistance on the way, he returned to the doorway to ensure that nobody moved the dagger. Joel was able to strip to the waist and bathe the wound in the kitchen sink. Lucky for him the tip of the knife had not penetrated far. He had sustained a nasty cut but it wasn't life threatening. Liam was able to tie a tea towel around Joel's shoulder to stop the blood.

The police arrived within ten minutes of being summoned. Two uniformed cops, one male, one female. A paramedic wasn't far behind them. The cops asked Joel for a description of his attacker. He gave them what he could. The guy was average height and size. Blonde colouring. Blue eyed. Perhaps in his mid-thirties. The officer got on his radio and requested assistance. He asked Liam what had happened, perhaps suspecting a domestic incident. Liam explained the situation to him and advised him to contact DI Berryman or DC Tyson in London. The female cop said she recognised him as Ryan Steadman from, 'Connaught Place'. When McAndrew had informed the cop of the events of the previous two weeks the young chap got onto one of his superiors and requested immediately CID assistance and a 'Scene of Crime' officer.

The paramedic put a couple of stiches into Joel's flesh and applied a bandage. Other than a lot of soreness he was okay, but the trauma of what had happened to him would stay with him for a while. The two uniformed cops stayed until they were relieved by two suits who arrived at eleven-fifteen.

DI Steve Nuttall was a big guy with a shaven head. His assistance was DC Samantha Lazenby. She was a rather plain looking woman in her early thirties with short hair and no make-up.

A member of a 'Scene of Crime' team arrived not long after them. He took several photographs of the dagger from different angles. He retrieved the knife and placed it into an evidence bag. Hopefully, the assailant had left his DNA on the weapon.

DI Nuttall asked all the pertinent questions. He listened to what Liam had to say. He told him everything. Nuttall was sharp as a tack. He quickly assessed the situation. The man who had firebombed his home in Kew that morning, must have followed him to Manchester, unless there was more than one attacker, or two working in tandem or independently of each other. Unlikely. The question was how he knew where Liam was this evening. The chance of the attacker following him from the office in Salford to this location was unlikely. Unless the taxi driver had disclosed this information, again unlikely. This seemed to come down to someone in the Head Office supplying the attacker with information. That narrowed the field down considerably. There was only Roger Hampson and Jill Lambourne who knew he was here. Nuttall and Lazenby considered this. Then Nuttall put in a late call to DI Berryman in London.

DI Berryman briefed Nuttall on the case so far. He revealed that the Metropolitan police had made a major breakthrough. They had in the past couple of hours interviewed the attendant at the petrol station in Brentford. She had provided them with a detailed description of the man who had purchased the petrol. When they compared this description to the one Joel had provided, then it was the same man. The arsonist was the attacker. There was a high probability that he was the man who had murdered Peter Newman. The weapon he had dropped may well have been the weapon he used to kill Peter Newman.

Great Manchester police would liaise with their colleagues in the capital. The results of the forensic tests on the knife would be given to colleagues in the Met as soon as the tests were complete. It still didn't answer the question of who had leaked the address of the flat to the attacker. This was the sixty-four-thousand-dollar question. The answer seemed to lie in the office of Roger Hampson and Jill Lambourne.

CHAPTER 10

In order to be on the scene both DI Berryman and DC Tyson caught the early morning shuttle flight up to Manchester. They met their colleagues, DI Nuttall and DC Lazenby at the office of the production company overlooking Salford Quays. They didn't inform the company of their visit. Meanwhile police in London had issued a description of a suspect wanted for the murder of Peter Newman. They believed he was the same man who set fire to the cottage in the early hours of the previous morning and attacked Joel Braviro last night.

On arrival at the office in Salford the police said they wished to speak to Roger Hampson. Hampson was surprised to see the police in the office. He never envisaged that the enquiry would pitch up here. When asked if he had spoken to anyone about the whereabouts of Liam he said he hadn't. Once the detectives had spoken to him, they sought Jill Lambourne. She was adamant that she hadn't spoken to anyone outside of the organisation about the problems Liam was having. It was strictly against company policy to speak to the press or anyone about any member of the company or any actor or actress in any of the company's productions. The only other person who knew where Liam was staying was her assistant. A woman of twenty-eight-years-of-age called Amanda Clarkson. When the officers asked to speak to her Lambourne told them that she was out of the office. She had been despatched to visit Liam to give him a card and a gift that colleagues had bought for him.

DC Tyson asked if it was normal company policy for staff to pay visits to soap actors in work time. Lambourne said it was nothing out of the ordinary.

It was DI Nuttall who quizzed both Hampson and Lambourne about their colleague. It was Lambourne who revealed that Clarkson was dating an eastern European man from Latvia. Nuttall asked her if she could describe the guy. She couldn't and neither could Hampson. The police asked if there was anyone who could. Lambourne said that Clarkson had a photograph of the chap on her desk. Nuttall asked her to get it. A minute later she returned with a picture frame in her hand. She showed it to the detectives. The man in the photograph fitted the description of the man they were looking for. Fair complexion. Eastern European features. Short fair hair. Slim face. Thin cheeks. Prominent cheek bones. Blue eyes.

DI Nuttall looked to his colleagues. "Quick someone contact McAndrew," he advised. "Tell him to be on his guard." He looked to Jill Lambourne. "When did she leave?" he asked.

"About fifteen minutes ago," she replied.

"What's going on?" Hampson asked.

"This could be the man who murdered Peter Newman and tried to kill Liam yesterday and attacked Joel Braviro last night."

Hampson put his hands to his face.

DC Tyson took his smart phone. He found Liam's number and hit the dial. It rang for five or six times before going to voice mail. "No answer," he said.

"Let's go to the flat," said Nuttall. The four officers, two from the Met, two from the GMP left the office and quickly made their way outside. They all got into Nuttall's car and headed the four miles towards Piccadilly.

Liam was startled by the knock at the door. He wasn't expecting anyone. It was just after ten-thirty. Joel had gone out to visit a local NHS walk-in centre to have the bandage changed. Liam had chosen to keep his head down. He had turned his mobile phone off.

He gingerly approached the front door to the flat. "Who is it?" he asked, through the door.

"It's Amanda Clarkson. From the company," came the response from the female at the other side of the door. "I've a gift for you. From colleagues in the production office."

He opened the door on the chain and peered through the opening. He clapped his eyes on a tall, slim woman in a nice peach, two-piece suit, holding a shiny gift bag in her hand. He recognised her from his previous visit to the company HQ. He recalled that she was the one who had copied the letters for Roger Hampson. She must have had the four-digit security code to get into the building.

"Come in," he said as he slipped the chain off and opened the door wide.

She smiled as she stepped into the flat. "How are you?" she asked.

"All right," he replied. "Come in and make yourself at home," he added.

She stepped into the lounge. She was quite an attractive girl. Long mousey blonde hair around her shoulders. Slim figure. Tall. Sparkling eyes. The hem of her pencil skirt was just above her knees. Nice legs in stockings. A pearl necklace around her neck. Gold earrings. Not too much make-up.

She came into the lounge. She had a shiny black shoulder bag on her shoulder as well as the gift bag in her hand. She looked towards the open balcony and admired the view over the railway tracks going into Piccadilly station.

"It's very kind of people to buy me something," he said.

She seemed not to hear him and continued to gaze through the window door at the balcony. Then she opened the bag and extracted a large bottle of Moet-Chandon, and a box of expensive chocolates. She put them on the coffee table, then she stepped onto the balcony. He followed her outside onto the balcony. The sun had come out and was now beaming into the flat to provide it with a pleasant warm radiance.

"Thank you very much..."

"Amanda," she said, looking at him for a few seconds more than necessary. She gave him a smile. She leant against the balcony railing and took in the view of the activity in the railway station. A Virgin Express train was just pulling into the station, passing one going in the opposite direction. Far in the distance the roof of the Etihad Stadium was visible.

"Is your partner here?" she asked.

"No. He's gone out," he replied.

She looked at him through concerned eyes. "We heard about it, this morning." She glanced back at the bottle of champagne and the box of chocolates.

He stepped to within a few feet of her and looked down to the ground, seven floors below. He didn't mind heights. She turned her head to look at him. The breeze caught her hair to blow strands across her face. She put her hair back and pulled it tight. Her eyes were nice. Captivating. She seemed to be flirting with him. Playing a cute game. Maybe she thought she could turn him. Maybe he was bi-sexual. Rumour had it that he swung both ways. Might she be trying to find out if it was true. She was coming onto him.

He placed his hands on the railing in front of him and rested against it. She was just a couple of feet to his side. He noticed that she had crossed her legs and was toying with the string of pearls around her neck. Turning them over and over. Her boobs under the silk blouse were in a perfect proportion. He looked at her and smiled.

"What do you do at…" He never finished the sentence as she forced herself on him. He assumed she was trying to kiss him, but her arms were at a funny angle. She wasn't trying to so much as hug him but force him over the edge of the railing. She was strong and had some power behind her. He wanted to say something on the lines of, *if you want to kiss then I don't mind*. But her mouth was nowhere near is. It quickly dawned on him that she wasn't trying to kiss him but force him over the railing. He gritted his teeth. He could smell her scent and feel her breath on him. His back was cutting into the edge of the railing. He looked down to the ground below. He managed to get hold of her wrists and force her back. She fought back. Just then he was aware of people inside the flat. The sound of rushing feet on the floor combined with the sound of voices. He saw DI Berryman, Tyson and Nuttall quickly coming through the sliding door and onto the balcony. They made straight for Amanda Clarkson and yanked her off him. Their combined force soon had her under control. It was DI Nuttall who took hold of Liam's shoulders and pulled him back upright. He was never in much danger of going over the edge of the balcony, but the sense of relief flowing through his veins was near to euphoric.

    The girl was dragged kicking and screaming through the door and into the lounge, where she was quickly subdued. DI Nuttall returned. He brought Liam inside the room and ensured that the sliding door was closed. He had survived again.

    The three male officers were tightly assembled around the girl as they shepherded her out of the front door into the internal corridor. In the struggle her pearl necklace snapped so tiny pearls were bouncing all around the floor like the contents of a broken pinball machine. She was soon being manhandled and taken out of the front door of the apartment by DI Nuttall and Lazenby.

Liam went to the sofa and fell onto it. He blew out a massive sigh and breathed in a deep gulp of fresh air. His eyes fell onto the champagne and the box of chocolates. Then he looked at DI Berryman. "Anyone care to tell me what's going on?" he asked.

Tyson looked at Berryman. Berryman looked at Tyson. Neither of them wanted to say anything, because the truth was that they didn't know.

When Joel returned from the medical centre one hour later he was met by the sight of a uniformed police officer standing at the front door to the flat. Once he had received the okay to enter he asked Liam what the hell was going on.

Liam looked at him and said, "You wouldn't believe it if I told you." Joel clapped his eyes on the bottle of champagne. Who...?

"Don't ask," said Liam.

It was around three in the afternoon when DI Berryman and DI Nuttall came back to the flat to chat to Liam. They made themselves comfortable in the lounge. Joel poured them both a cold drink each. In the main it was DI Nuttall who explained what was going on. What he had to say was eye opening to say the least. Amanda Clarkson had been questioned. After initial resistance she had agreed to cooperate.

She had given them an address of a house in Wythenshawe, south Manchester where her boyfriend could be found. DI Berryman said local police were going around there to arrest him as we speak. She had named her boyfriend has Eric Janson. The crazy thing is that Eric Janson happened to be Andrea Janson's older brother. The actress who played Marie the Polish waitress in, 'Connaught Place'.

Amanda had given Eric Janson information about Liam and Peter Newman. Such as their addresses and other classified information. Information she had taken from the company files.

He had taken it upon himself to conduct a one-man campaign of hate against Liam in order to protect his sister. The man was clearly insane. He wasn't playing with a full deck. To him the soap wasn't pretend, it was real life. When Ryan Steadman bossed Marie about it was as if it was real. It wasn't a soap opera. Clarkson had become embroiled in the plot and was clearly unhinged herself. She admitted that she was infatuated with Liam but on learning that he was gay and unavailable to her she began to imagine all kinds of ways she could hurt him.

Police were seeking Andrea Janson to ask her about her brother and to establish whether she was involved. Liam felt sorry for Andrea. It wasn't her fault that her brother was barking mad.

When Liam McAndrew appeared in the newspapers and on the TV shows Eric Janson took it as a personal insult. There was also a possibility that Amanda Clarkson had heard the whispers about changes in personal in the soap and had told Eric. He took it on himself to help his sister achieve soap stardom. If Ryan Steadman was written out of the soap then perhaps his sister would become the manager of 'The Winery'. It was bizarre. Crazy. Her ascent up the greasy pole could be achieved with Ryan Steadman out of the way.

What Amanda Clarkson's role was never truly explained to McAndrew. Later she was sectioned under the Mental Health Act and diagnosed with a personality disorder.

After a siege lasting a couple of hours police raided the house in Wythenshawe and found Eric Janson hiding in a cupboard. He was arrested on suspicion of the murder of Peter Newman. His sister swore blind that she didn't know anything about her brother's rampage.

Within the Production Company an internal investigation led by the Chief Executive officer took place. The result was that Roger Hampson and Jill Lambourne were shunted sideways. A new head of production, an old school guy by the name of Barry Lincoln was drafted in.

The idea of replacing the older members of the cast was dropped. Lincoln was keen to keep the old guard and move away from the idea of new blood. After all, the market research conducted by the pollsters revealed that the audience preferred the established characters to new ones.

Sadly, through no fault of her own, Andrea Janson was axed from the show, though she was soon working again in the theatre. Roger Hampson left the company four months later to take up a post with a rival company. As a mark of their respect and to say sorry for all the problems he had had to endure Liam received a heartfelt apology. Negotiations about a new contract took place in early October. Liam agreed to a new year three deal worth half a million pounds, with add-ons.

Despite what had happened to him he came out of it smelling of roses. The crazy thing was that none of this was ever reported in the press. Only those in the know knew what really had gone on.

It was perhaps difficult to believe, but Liam never wanted the publicity in the first place. And who said that soap scripts were far-fetched? True life was far more bizarre. A soap script could never begin to imitate real life?

The End

Printed in Poland
by Amazon Fulfillment
Poland Sp. z o.o., Wrocław